Rucksack Tales

Stories from The Lakes

J M Moore

Rucksack Tales
Stories from The Lakes

First published in 2016
J.M. Moore

Copyright © J.M. Moore 2016

ISBN 978-1537409573

Dedication

I would like to say thanks to all my friends for their unswerving support, without their encouragement I would not have continued. I would particularly like to thank Helen who has endured years of tweaks, re-writes and edits with a placid patience beyond the call of duty.

Renegade Writing Group also deserve thanks – for the harshest critics are sometimes the best! I have learned much from this group and wouldn't have created this work without their input.

Shirley Knight for the bookcover photo of me and the picture in Wannabe Sam.

Thank you Val Wood for recognising the story-teller in me. I would not have come this far without your faith.

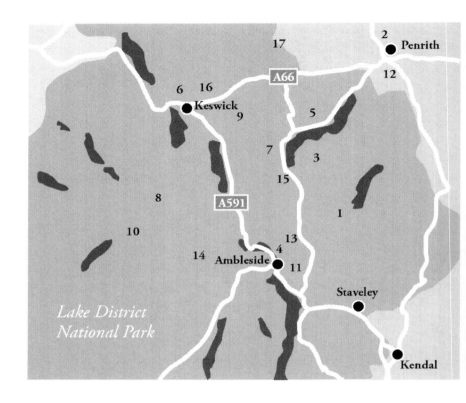

Contents

24 Hours

Across the broad back of High Street, I caught a glimpse of the beacon. It stood proud and aloof, very much alone and I was grateful for the sight of it. I imagined it to be female, a stalwart, never giving in to the ravages of time or weather, brave and upright like a warrior, perhaps named Boudica? I allowed my thoughts to wander, swayed by the history of the place. I needed to think of something, anything other than work. I estimated thirty minutes to reach her, it was a fair guess and my pace was fast: it was too cold to hang about on that frosty morn.

She was a commanding sight and appeared and disappeared as I made my way high up along the popular Roman road. Cloud enveloped me, mist swirled and changed its mind, teased and led me along sheep trods I shouldn't have been on, but I needed the space after an atrocious week and I embraced the solitude. A quiet day on the fells was all I needed to restore my equilibrium. I wiped my face free of moisture as I was sucked further into the grey. I shrugged. It wasn't for the faint-hearted. The snow had almost gone save for pockets here and there, particularly anything north-facing. I was glad of my new jacket. Lime like spring and right now, that seemed a long way off.

I knew Thornthwaite was one of the tallest cairns in The Lakes. Standing at 14' high, I couldn't begin to guess its girth. Yet that morning it managed to look ethereal, ghost-like in its blue hue, a wisp of cloud skulked around its base and I walked purposefully towards it with more than a flicker of trepidation. Under normal conditions, it would have been a simple yomp, but the clag hit fast and smudged and blurred my view. It wasn't often I was unnerved. I needed to get a grip.

Racecourse Hill, the flat summit, sparked my imagination and I strode across where ancient games were played and the strong felled the weak. I imagined horses and mounts materialising through the vapour, clashing swords, blood, and aggression. Not unlike work this last week, I snorted at the irony. It was spooky though and I distracted myself thinking I'd take a metal detector next time, perhaps find a buckle or an amulet? It was wishful thinking, I'd never carry one up there and I discarded my childish thoughts and concentrated on the more prosaic, whether I should descend the aptly named Gray Crag. I wondered if it would tempt fate knowing the summit was strewn with slithers of protruding rock, standing on end like miniature gravestones. My head was not in the right place. Work had messed me up. I knew I needed to relax. Too many deadlines. Not enough time. I didn't need the pressure. Work was intruding once again and I forced myself to think of the feet that walked the same way hundreds of years before me, tramping over fells to where? Hardknott Fort? It was a good distraction, so much so, I was startled when I heard voices; as yet, I couldn't see anything. Whoever was at the beacon was having a row and the relief of knowing people were about evaporated as fast as the clouds. Peace was shattered. I'd had enough of the ranting and raving at work.

'You bloody well did!' A female voice rose, high pitched. Accusing.

'I did not! I've told you time after time!' A male. A bellow from the gut.

'You were seen with her! You can't deny it, you bastard! You were seen!'

Spitting feathers or what? Crikey. I slowed. I wasn't sure whether to cough, let them know I was approaching. They started again.

'That's absolute bollocks!'

'Yeah, I'm sure it was! Yours!'

'I'm not having this!'

'That's right, run away...when the going gets tough...'

Lordy, lordy, it wasn't what I needed. How dare they rant when I'd come up here for peace and reflection? I caught another glimpse of the silhouetted figures before the cloud embraced them. They shoved each other, her turn, his turn, her turn. She was pushing harder than him. I almost laughed. It was all so surreal and

I thought about hanging back from this intensely private scene. I really wasn't sure what to do. I'd been looking forward to reaching the beacon, eating my lunch in peace with the hope of an occasional view, but this wasn't how I thought it would turn out. Cloud smothered me again and their voices became muted and dull. All sound was now lost. I desperately wanted the cloud to lift as I was drawn inexorably into their drama and admittedly wanted the volume up. I wanted the details. I quickened my pace and was rewarded with a new volley. The gloves were off. It was an extraordinary exchange, enough to make me cringe. I waited. Hung back a moment. It was awful, yet I realised – much as we dislike the racket – a part of us enjoys the little snoop and I smiled wryly as I strained to hear more. There was one final screech of blind fury and it frightened the hell out of me.

There was nothing more to be heard. Nothing. When I reached the beacon, there wasn't a sign of them, not a trace. It was like I'd imagined it all and I breathed a sigh of relief, grateful they were gone. Perhaps the mountain was messing with my head. I flopped beneath the dry-stone wall, turned to face the way I'd just come. Southwards, there was a fleeting glimpse of the multi-cairned Ill Bell and a glimpse had to satisfy; the mist was in a mischievous mood today and danced a dance to its own tune. I sat a while; I was well-wrapped up and the lichened wall afforded enough shelter. I hadn't seen a soul all day, except for the argumentative two-some. I stretched out my legs. I could relax now.

The coffee cup was half-way to my mouth when I heard the groan. At first I thought it was a Herdy, but the second moan convinced me it wasn't an animal and I stood, better to locate the sound. I stepped through the gap in the wall and there he was sprawled on rimed rock, hidden the other side of the beacon. I'd missed him entirely. I slithered down towards him, repulsed by his mashed features but managed to mumble what I hoped were words of comfort, 'Hey, Jen's here. It's going to be okay. Can you hear me? Hello? Hello?'

No response. I stood too quickly, slipped and steadied myself. I looked around for any emerging shape, anyone who might be near but there was no one. 'Hello? Hello?' I cupped my hands to my mouth and yelled, but was greeted with silence. The footpath gave no clues; prints were compacted, all snow flattened by earlier feet. I bent down and put my arm under his head. 'Stay still,' I said as sticky brown lumps smudged my sleeve, unwelcome smears on my jacket. It was all over my hands too. I don't like blood and I wiped my hands down the rock, shuddering at the colour and its stickiness. His head didn't look good, but then he surprised me by trying to move so I pulled out my spare fleece and packed it under his head, told him to stay still and blew on his hands. He'd taken his gloves off but they were close by and I tried unsuccessfully to stuff his frozen fingers in. He mumbled again something like, 'I never did...' before lapsing into semi-consciousness.

'Sshh. Stay still,' I said as I unfurled a foil blanket and tucked him up. I got on the phone to the emergency services. He was out for the count but I continued to talk to him, kneeling in close to his ear, hoping his brain would compute that a helicopter was on its way. Help would be with him soon.

As I waited, the mist lifted and in minutes there was a glorious jet-trailed azure sky. It raised my spirits no end. Perhaps this was an omen all would end well? The chopper would be able to land. The last of the melting snow was making everywhere sparkle and water droplets dripped and formed new pools. I dug out my sunglasses. A crow fluttered on the beacon, cocked its head and cawed. It flew off as the deep, thrilling woc-a-choc of the rescue helicopter thundered out its presence. I could just about make it out in the shadow of the fellside. I waved and waved with a demonic passion. I was sure they'd seen me but it felt like the right thing to do. It would be minutes to touch down.

After a brief explanation of what I'd heard and seen that morning, I knew I was in danger of getting in their way and decided to carry on my walk. There wasn't any point in hanging around further. I don't think anyone even noticed me go, but I wished I'd got his name so I could ring the hospital, check if he was okay.

The man's name turned out to be John Mansfield. The day I met John was not my best. Understatement of the year. I arrived home at 7pm, having nipped in to Morrison's on the way home. I was shattered and my meal for one and bottle of Pinot whipped from the chilled counter would suit me well. But, I didn't even get the bags out of the boot of my car before I was pounced on by the police. I failed to convince them I could go into the station after I'd eaten. I was escorted. It was so embarrassing but I really couldn't wait to tell the girls on Monday. What can you do when they ask you to help with their enquiries? I wasn't sure what I could help with but thought it best to comply with whatever.

****

'Miss Hepburn, did you pick up any of his things?'

'I'm sorry?' I was seated in what I thought was an interrogation room. The walls were plain, no posters or pictures, nothing to add interest or distraction. I was obviously meant to pay attention to the question.

'Any of his belongings?' The young, spotty man stared hard at me. It was meant to make me uncomfortable and it was working. The pause was long. The procedure new to me, a bit like on television I supposed.

'Miss Hepburn. Listen carefully. Did you, or did you not, take his wallet?' I felt like I was his first interrogation, like he was practising on me and I imagined him spending his evenings with Horlicks and Spider-Man comics. It made me feel better. I was astounded, I'd helped the man out and now I was asked if I'd helped myself!

'No of course I didn't!' I wanted to add more but thought I'd better keep quiet. This was just stupid. Apparently John had no memory of the incident. They found out who he was from an emergency tag buried deep in his rucksack.

'John doesn't have a partner, doesn't have a girlfriend; his mother would know as he moved back in with her three weeks ago,' he tilted his head sideways. 'So!' he smacked his lips. 'We are looking into things, Miss Hepburn. We talked to Mr Mansfield, but he was still a bit fu...' he squirmed, decided on a politer term, 'mixed up before the hospital put him into an induced coma,' the officer coughed and carried on. 'Perhaps he will be able to tell us more in time — that's if he comes out of it okay.' This guy was too young for the role; he was still trying to impress me.

'Did you speak to Mr Mansfield prior to calling the services? Are you sure you don't know him? It seems unusual a young woman like yourself would wander the fells all alone on such a murky day.' A flicker of a smirk spread across his face. I would have liked to know what the women PCs made of his cocky little stance.

I took a deep breath; he obviously didn't understand me or my sort and I warned myself not to rise to the bait. 'No. I've told you what happened. I was on a walk, minding my own business and heard this couple having a row. It was very misty up there; you know what it's like, one minute you can see and the next you can't.' I didn't know if he understood and I found myself rattling on from the sheer anxiety of sitting in a police room. 'Well, I heard them shouting at each other. I resented it at first then found it mildly amusing in a just my kind of luck way but when I sat down at the cairn I thought I was completely on my tod until I heard him moan. It was really strange. I thought it was a sheep at first.' Was I saying too much? Did I need a solicitor? I didn't even watch crime on TV! Well, very little so as not to count. I wondered if I should be saying No Comment after every question he threw at me. I realised I was looking guilty just by being me. 'And that's it! That's what happened.' I sat back in my seat and folded my arms. 'I've never met him before in my life!' I heard the wobble in my voice and wondered if that in itself was incriminating. I needed my dad.

******

They left me in a side room for ages without a clue as to what was going on. I didn't even catch the whiff of a teabag. It wasn't looking good. Grim faces peered at me through the glass panel in the door; muted voices troubled me. Their eyes said they had seen it a thousand times before. I was expecting to be charged. It was another hour before someone came in and sat opposite. I was starving!

'We have had some concerns, Miss Hepburn.' The officer threw a sheaf of papers on the table. 'Why did you leave the scene so quickly?' I hadn't seen this guy before; he was older, wiser, sharper, yet I sensed he was weary. Perhaps due for retirement. Was this the Good Cop or the Bad Cop?

'I don't understand. I just don't know what's the big deal?' I really didn't. 'Scene?' I shook my head, 'I thought I was in the way of the rescue guys and so set off to get home. I didn't think I needed to hang around. I thought I'd get away, leave things to the experts.'

I didn't like the look of this guy at all; he was bald, shiny. He wiped his brow with a crumpled handkerchief. I went to speak but changed my mind. He noticed.

'You were about to say something?'

'No. I just want to go home. That's all.'

He scratched at his head with a pencil, all the while rocking slowly back on his chair. It needed WD40, it was a squeaker. The stare penetrated deep. I wanted to laugh knowing it was my usual reaction to serious things and wetted my lips which I also knew was a nervous thing. Oh heck I could hear my mum's voice telling me to grow up! I concentrated on the man before me; he looked hard as nails, his stare terrifying. He breathed in long and slow, relishing the control he believed he had over me. I wanted that glass of Pinot more than anything else in the world.

'We talked to his mum this morning.' He indicated somewhere vaguely towards town with a nod of his head. 'Up at the hospital. She's an upset old lady. Are you sure you don't want to tell us a little more, Miss Hepburn?'

I didn't like how he said my surname; he managed to inject malice, doubt, cynicism, scorn, the list went on — all into one word! It felt like another case of the strong felling the weak and I wished I was back on High Street, wished I'd never heard the couple. Wished I'd never got involved. I needed to think like a warrior, like a strong woman, but I felt like the condemned with his waggling finger too close to my face. He fended off my further questions until he'd said his piece.

'We have a lot to find out about you Miss Hepburn, in the meantime we have the small matter of taking your fingerprints. We may let you out tomorrow. Then again, maybe not.'

All Passion Unspent

Arnold took his chance, thinking Audrey would be very pleased if he'd been productive whilst she was at flower arranging. He lifted the Mundy hammer and gave it a good swing. Nothing budged except dust and distemper which flaked and floated gently to damp, earthen floor. He coughed, wiped his nose and took another swing before realising it was going to be a lot harder than he thought to create a new and useable space. He fished out a rag from his back pocket, blew his nose before using the same cloth to wipe away fine cobwebs and took another calculated swing in the confined space. Rhythm was good. Rhythm was right. There would be plenty of rhythm from his members when he finished sorting their new dungeon. He chuckled until he cried, wiped his eyes on that same cloth and continued with the hammer. Whump. Whump. Whump.

On spotting something, he sat back on his haunches, glad of the rest, glad to get his breathing back under control and said aloud, 'Well now, what have we here?'

He twirled his goatee, pondered on what he could see and smiled a secret smile. So much potential.

An irregular gap of about two brick sizes crumbled away before him and intrigued, he thrust his arm through the void, feeling around with his fingers. Fumbling in the dark, groping in the empty space, he was unable to touch anything. However, barely within fingertip reach, he felt something flat, cold and smooth and therefore, he deduced, it was recent plaster, not as ancient as his own home. He surmised correctly that it was next door and best to be avoided. He didn't want to bash their wall by mistake. That would not do. As he pulled his hand back, it scraped on something jagged and he tugged at the offending piece. It pulled away easily and he peered at it before throwing it down in disgust. His finger oozed blood and he sucked away, licking every drop before moving his torch-light closer to the breach. He needed new batteries for it; it was too dim to see properly, but he peered anyway. They were always using batteries; they never seemed to have enough. He squinted in the dark, the gloom of the cellar revealed nothing new and he ran his thumb over broken laths, nodded and carried on. Ancient wattle and daub held no interest for him. He pulled more. A little bit of stone, a little bit of horse hair. A lot of debris. It was a shame it had to go. Tough titty, he chuckled. This was progress. His new guests would want something else entirely. He owed it to them. He chuckled again and licked his cracked lips, forgetting the dust contained centuries-old dung.

He carried on removing history piece by dusty piece and muttered about the terrace being so old. He shrugged and tugged at another and another, knowing full-well he was undoing ancient hand work. Hand work. He chuckled again. Audrey would be pleased.

The front door banged open and his Beloved rubbed her feet on the coir mat. He called to her, 'Hello love, I've made you some tea. How did tonight go?' He always had tea ready for her.

Audrey bustled in, pulled off her hat and placed her shopper full of silk flowers and ribbons in the Cupboard That Held Everything. Shoes tumbled out and into the hall and she expertly kicked them back in whilst patting her back-combed hair.

'I'll just get me coat off and I'll tell you all about it.' Without pausing for breath, she continued, 'Marge was there as usual; she creates weird stuff, all twists of twigs and twine and things. Too showy for my liking! She needs to get out more!' she laughed. 'Have we got any of those Jammy Dodgers left or have you scoffed them all?' She gave him a certain look; a look that always piqued his interest and it wasn't about the Jammy Dodgers either. She continued, 'Some of the others laugh about it, but I think she could be a bit like us...' her eyes glistened and she dropped her voice, indicated something with her head, mouthing, 'well, you know...' He knew.

'Is she?' Audrey had his attention.

'Well, she could be. I haven't sussed her out yet, but I pick up on these things. You know I get a feel for them,' Audrey giggled, barely able to contain herself. 'She had one of those rubbery bracelets with letters on.' Her voice dropped again, 'I don't know, I could be jumping the gun...but then again, it seems a bit obvious to me when you have a certain combination of letters.'

Arnold blew on his tea, a far-away look in his eye and chuckled some more. He said, 'I know you are better at spotting them than me.' He watched for a reaction from his wife of 52 years and felt those familiar stirrings.

Audrey settled into her wing chair and said, 'Don't you get that look in your eye Arnie, I'm buggered!' Clapping her hands she fell back in her chair and waggling her raised feet at him, she knew he wouldn't mind catching sight of her knickers. Tears of laughter rolled down four creased cheeks. Old jokes were best shared.

Moving to the sink, he washed, she dried, before taking the creaky stairs to the top floor. Together they rolled the Damask cover down the bed, he on one side, she on the other and in unison placed the fat sausage on the wicker blanket box.

'What do you fancy tonight, love?' Arnold asked, reaching for the remote.

'I don't know, we need to get something new. I've watched everything ten times over. I'm fed up of Lust and Lashes; we need to buy something fresh.'

'How about Virgin On The Ridiculous? You always enjoy that.' Audrey gave him a bored look before crossing her arms to lift her peach slip expertly over her shoulders. Arnold ignored the bingo wings, concentrating on her other wobbly bits which never failed to delight. Like the butterfly emerging from a chrysalis, what she revealed was far more enticing. On went ruby red, satin and black lace. She looked at him and he thought her eyes looked steely, cold, so different from her public mask. She could flip in seconds and it never failed to excite him.

'Oh Audrey. My lovely, lovely Mistress.' Arnold dropped to the floor like a damaged fledgling and Audrey, once more, raked her stiletto down his scarred spine. He was in heaven. Sort of.

******

It was two days later when Arnold went back into the cellar. The wall was coming down fairly quickly; in fact it was coming down in huge chunks of its own accord and the more that fell naturally — the better! Blackpool was coming up fast. It was an annual event and he'd promised faithfully that he would have the cellar — their Dungeon of Dreams — ready so they could invite new members, but it was tiring work. In fact, it was wearing him out and he needed energy, energy to keep his wife entertained. He scratched his head. He needed to come up with a ruse. What if he said there was a rat? Audrey hated the things. What if he pretended there was one in the cellar? It would give him a little bit of time off. And so that is what he did. He told her he would put poison down and it would need a good few days to make sure the beastie had eaten it. It was all fibs of course — but he was knackered!

Audrey had no truck with rats and blocked the access to the cellar with a large, damp towel. Arnold wasn't sure why she dampened it but if it made her happy, he said nothing except to mention large yellow incisors which he knew did nothing to help Audrey's nerves. Arnold was despatched to get the job done as quickly as possible.

After a couple of hours of seeking out poison in Penrith, he ducked into the cellar saying, 'I'll be back as soon as I'm done.' Audrey shuddered and slammed the cellar door after him, nudging the towel into place. Half an hour later he emerged, covered in dust, saying he'd had enough for the day and needed a cup of tea. He asked if Audrey wanted a peek, at which she turned her back, muttered something about 'over her dead body' and put the kettle on. Before flicking the switch, she went back to the door and made sure the towel was tucked well in place.

'Have we got anyone coming tonight?' He knew the impact his words would have on his Beloved and watched Audrey perk up, her eyes glistened with anticipation.

She licked her lips, 'Only the regulars. We could do with some new flesh.' She sighed longingly and wiped the remnants of custard creams from around her mouth. 'How long before the room is finished?' Arnold squirmed and lied about rats and the length of time it took for poison to work. He hoped the wall would hold in place until they returned from Blackpool; if it fell down it would be more difficult to bag-up.

'Do you want to come and have a look?' He knew she wouldn't. His con was perfect for a few days rest. 'It's hard work. I want it finished just as much as you do my love, but these things can't be hurried. They have to be done properly. It's going to take time...and that bloody great rat...well, we need to make sure it's taken the bait...' he didn't need to add more.

'Time? You said we would have it done before the convention!' Audrey shrieked above the washing machine as it vibrated across the lino. 'You said it would be ready!'

Arnold shrank under her bulging eyes and said, 'I'm sorry Mistress Audrey. I'm sorry, but the rat has made all the difference to my time schedule. I'll work extra hard when we come back. I promise, Mistress.'

Neither moved, not quite knowing what to say. The disappointment on Audrey's face saddened him, but they were distracted by someone at the front door. It was the postman and the plop of a parcel lifted the mood. Both moved at once. They had been expecting a delivery.

Arnold held back, let his wife take control and said, 'Go on. You open it,' and peered over her shoulder, his Adam's Apple bobbing in delicious anticipation.

Audrey wiped her chin of saliva and tugged at the brown sealing tape; it tightened and she lost patience, tearing it with her teeth.

'Here, use the scissors dear. Be careful, you don't want to damage them.'

Audrey snatched at the scissors, licking her lips when she opened the lid. Arnold thought her eyes never looked lovelier. Arnold knew that look well. He watched her move closer to the window where she held aloft the promise of control. She twirled fluffy red handcuffs above her head and giggled, 'I like the Swarovski crystals don't you? It's a nice touch. Only the best for our guests.'

'Nothing but the best love. Nothing but the best.'

******

The convention was held in Blackpool and was an annual treat for Arnold and Audrey. They had been going for years and greeted friends, old and new. Of course they knew their matching T-shirts made them stand out. She managed to convince Arnold that 'Blackpool or Bust' with a pair of boobs on the front was not right for their image and they settled on, 'Up For It' which Audrey thought was much more tasteful. They felt like celebrities. This was their 'thing', their 'world' and they wouldn't miss it for all the tea in China. They were overjoyed with their purchases of gadgets and gizmos, often coming home with freebies or feelies as Audrey liked to call them. Testing them would be fun.

Something caught Audrey's attention and she pointed across the heads, 'Look, Justin has got a new stand! We need to get over there!'

'Where?'

'Over there! Number 69!' They chuckled like teenagers who have just discovered sex and pushed through the throng, pressed against flesh. Audrey read Arnold's mind as he cupped a young bum before him.

Justin was as camp as camp could be. He took pride in being billed the Biggest Bitch in Blackpool. His radio show was known far and wide. He had one long blonde plait, brought forward over his left shoulder, always tied with a black bow. He could sashay for Britain. Always described as a character by anyone who came across him, his flamboyance was only outdone by the famous lights themselves. Everyone knew he was gay, but not everyone knew he adored Arnold and Audrey.

'Hello, Darlings! My most favourite people in the entire world!' Justin greeted them with triple air kisses and ushered them behind the scenes where they drank warm penile coladas and he showed them his latest toys and tricks.

'You need one of these!' He held up a pink whirling thing he said could be filled with gel for extra sensation. Audrey laughed and said they had worn out two already!

He tried hard to sell them a black vibrator but they declined, saying they'd bought enough. To keep him straight, (a phrase Arnold found very amusing) they bought plastic tape and bartered for an ex-demonstrator leather crop. They knew they had a bargain; there was only a little bit of fraying on the handle and at least they knew where it had been!

Three large drinks later and they meandered to the next stall, Arnold's free hand never leaving Audrey's arm. Clutching over-loaded plastic bags, they pushed their way through the masses until Audrey stopped dead, she'd spotted something and pointed. She could hardly get the words out.

'Look! They sell those BDSM bracelets! That's what Marge's looked like!'

'You're joking! Wouldn't it be a bit unusual for someone at flower arranging to wear something like that? Maybe you should talk to her? Maybe she is desperate — to make it that obvious!'

Audrey nodded in acknowledgement, 'I don't know. I could give her one of these leaflets I suppose, see what her reaction is. You have to be careful; Cumbria can cast you out very quickly. I've seen it happen.' She looked at her watch before saying, 'We have three-quarters of an hour before we catch the bus home. Come on let's do those last few stands before the stampede to get out.'

******

They left before the rush and as they waited in the queue for the No 47, Audrey reminded Arnold to zip his coat up as there were some funny folk about. Passes were flashed and they took their seats on the crowded bus as it inched through Blackpool's rush hour. The Illuminations flickered over their faces as they dozed on the way home.

Back on local territory, the taxi driver explained he couldn't take them down their street as there'd been an incident. It was cordoned off.

'Oh! What sort of an incident?' Arnold stretched forward in his seat.

'I don't know but there were three police cars earlier and the road was sealed off. Looked serious. Alarms were going off at the bank, something about a break-in. They had the guys in black, you know, wearing caps 'n guns. I think they were guns.

I'll bet it's the Romanians again. Honestly...the stories I hear. One guy...'

'Stop here!' Audrey commanded as she peered through the window. 'We can trundle the suitcases along the alley. Pay the man will you? Ooh heck, it's close to our house.' Audrey was on the edge of her seat trying to see what was going on through the finger-smudged window. Arnold fumbled for coins.

'Six-twenty, six-thirty, six-pounds, forty. Here, make it six-fifty. Keep the change.'

The driver didn't say goodbye. He looked at the coins in his hand, glanced up at the couple as they clambered out of the cab, shook his head and drove off.

Audrey's progress was blocked by tape. She went to lift it, explaining it was her house and was promptly arrested. Arnold went to open his mouth and was also taken in for questioning.

Their neighbour, (Marge of the twitchy curtains and dubious bracelet), kindly offered to put them up overnight as Audrey and Arnold were effectively without their home. 'Substantial alterations' had to be made in their cellar after the wall came tumbling down and set off the alarm. Audrey couldn't bear to look at Marge over her superior Seville marmalade any longer; smug shades of flower-arranging-one-up-man-ship still niggled and she said she'd had enough and they were leaving.

'Pronto Arnold. Pronto.' To Marge she sniffed, 'I don't know why you look so self-satisfied all the time. I've seen your bracelet! You can't be that bloody satisfied or you wouldn't need to advertise!' Audrey rounded on the very shocked Marge.

'I've no idea what you are talking about.' Marge was genuinely confused.

'Your BDSM bracelet! You're the same as us. Go on admit it!' Arnold put a steadying hand out and Audrey shrugged him off with more force than necessary. 'Go on admit it!'

'I don't know what you think this is Audrey Grimshaw but if you look closely – yes...go on! It says Brian, David, Sarah, and Mandy. My four children! What did you think it meant?'

Audrey couldn't get out of the door fast enough.

The following morning, their mug shots were splashed across the local rag. It was time to move after 32 years of living next to the bank. Their sex lives and interests were flogged for all to see and they scurried away under cover of darkness using their local man with a van.

Marge tittered at the headline and settled down to pore over the evening paper's fine details. The headline screamed: Penrith Pensioners in Barclays Bonk Job. She thought it funny how you never really got to know your neighbours.

Beda's Silence

Under-valued and over-looked, Beda Fell, next to its mightier cousin, Place Fell, is trudged by few. Wainwright Baggers and those looking for solitude tramp its ridge, but most leave it be. This fell, like many, holds a secret, one I stumbled across by accident. I did think about going to the police but made the decision to leave it alone. Whether it was right or wrong – you can judge. My wife would have a fit if she knew what I'd stumbled across in that isolated, tucked away spot on such a cold day.

Looking back, I remember deer rutting close by, their lonely sound: unusual, distinctive, perhaps even mournful to my ears and it echoed down through the valley. Once adjusted to their language I could discern individual cries, but they were difficult to spot even with binoculars. Only their insistent call for a mate lets you into their world, lets you know they are there. At other times of the year you wouldn't know they existed, so silently do they live in their remote basin. I walked some more, it was early morning; I wanted to ensure I had the fell to myself and set off at 6.30. The Helvellyn range was hugged with a thick pervasive mist but I hoped this clagg, this fog, would burn off and I would be rewarded with the views. It was going to be a changeable day.

I'd stumbled upon the body when looking for somewhere private to answer nature's call. With Boredale to my right, I headed away from the summit and dropped down 50 metres or so. On this particular day there were a couple of noisy groups, so I went further away from the track in my desire to find a quiet spot. And there he was. Sat upright in an overhang; it was more of a cave really. Naturally, he frightened the life out of me; I'm no expert but I guessed he hadn't been there long at all. His head had slumped a little, but he was still in one piece, no animal or bird had touched him yet. I knew nothing about rates of decay for bodies but assumed the deed had been done within 24 hours. He had the right gear on. At first glance, it all looked rather expensive. His red woollen hat had an Alfred Wainwright badge, the distinctive little green rectangle and another, the gold one, had the number 214, the 'Completer's Badge'. I knew it would help identify him as a member of the society. His red jacket was of good quality – as were his boots. His rucksack lay upright next to him and poking out from the top was a drained scotch bottle, and on the ground, an empty pill bottle. For a moment, my heart went out to him. What possessed a guy to do that? What demons stalked him? I almost wanted to touch him, pat his arm, tell him it would be okay. I shook my head. What was I thinking? I stumbled out without reading the message propped on his lap.

I went back to my room in the B&B, threw my keys on the bed and fought a myriad of conflicting emotions. I was pissed off with myself for running away so quickly. I needed a shower but lay for a while and tried to visualise the wording on the wallet. I'd panicked and left the scene quickly, scared I'd throw up. My cowardice was embarrassing, but I consoled myself by saying most people would have run away, and yet for some reason I felt I should pay my respects to a fellow fell-walker and return. At least read the message! Should I? Shouldn't I? Should I leave it alone or ring the police?

I slammed the shower door harder than I meant to and let the hot water cascade over me for a long time before reaching for the shower gel. It felt good to linger but no matter how hard I scrubbed at myself, I just couldn't get the man's face out of my mind. I knew I was working myself into a lather, but it was no joke. I resolved to go back the next day and see Beda Bloke – as I came to think of him. I had to read the message. For reasons I still cannot fathom, I dismissed the emergency services and I knew I would return on my own ... the very next day.

It took a while to find the cave; the shadows altered the fell tops in that fascinating way I have come to love. I scrambled down a steep bit, dislodged stones and waited for them to stop slithering before swinging to the right. I wondered what had possessed me to find such a place just to go to the loo – but then I remembered it was because of the people. Today was much quieter. I swallowed hard. Here it was. Here he was. Sat, just like he was yesterday. What really stopped me in my tracks was the wording on the message propped up on his lap. He'd used a plastic wallet, the sort used to protect maps. Small, spidery capital letters spelled out his last message to the world. I felt sick and to be honest, a little afraid. As if a corpse could harm? I questioned why my stomach flipped and reminded myself to get a grip. It was only a body.

The words scrawled on scrap paper could just about be made out without touching the wallet. Condensation marred clarity. I didn't touch it, knowing I could potentially leave prints. It said, I CAME HERE TO BE ALONE. TO DIE ALONE. TO REMAIN ALONE. PLEASE RESPECT MY WISHES. LEAVE WELL ALONE.

What a sad little epitaph it was. I stumbled out once more, sat on a rock and took a deep breath. I threw my gloves down and rubbed hard at my face, took another deep breath. I would let him be. I would leave him alone as requested, yet I knew it would haunt me. Knew it would stay with me. People have rights, don't they? I'd heard about folks ending their lives this way; finding a quiet place in The Lakes and after downing a bottle, letting the cold do its work. Dying in a place they loved. I shuddered and struggled with the ethics of right and wrong. What about family back home? If he had any? Wouldn't they want to know?

I felt relief on making my decision. It was not my responsibility to notify anyone. I would leave the little hiding place as I found it. Undisturbed. It was no deeper than five feet and not much higher than four. Beda Bloke was still sitting upright, not slumped but propped. He could stay there. Not my problem. I decided I'd have a stiff whisky at The White Lion. If I walked briskly, it would take under an hour. I was in need of a drink. It was too late for panic but my stomach was in knots the more I thought of him.

******

I was drawn to lonely Beda Fell, that quiet, enchanting ridge some months later, once more craving solitude but, not surprisingly, Beda Bloke wouldn't leave my mind. I didn't want to try and find the cave. I really didn't want to know. I assumed he would have been found by now as Beda isn't exactly remote, not being far from the lovely village of Patterdale. I distracted myself with thoughts of St Patrick recalling why the village was named after him. I vowed to go to the holy well and cross myself with water for not reporting my discovery. I amused myself with such thoughts as I walked to the summit, but I was disappointed to find there were three people hovering near the cairn, their laughter filtered towards me and I was irritated they too were up so early and spoiling the peace. The only sound I wanted to hear was deer or Herdwick sheep but I was drawn into chatter with them, the usual stuff.

'Where have you come from?'

'Did you see the deer near Angle Pike?'

'Are you doing the C2C?'

The couple nattered on but the guy on his own nodded an acknowledgement and carried on eating his flapjack, his coffee steaming close by.

The air pressure had changed and dark clouds were approaching fast. A threatening bank of black clagg was minutes away from cloaking us. The man and woman scuttled off quickly, making excited noises, laughing as they ran, saying something about 'not getting caught out' and I reached into my rucksack for waterproofs as fast as I could. The man stood and put his jacket on adding, 'Any second that's going to hit us,' and he was right; it took less than a minute to reach us. We were enveloped in a fine swathe of moisture, the sort that soaked through anything that wasn't waterproof, yet the air was still, silent.

'Do you mind if I walk with you?' he asked, 'Two heads are better than one in this pea-souper.' The guy unnerved me as he pulled on a red jacket. Dammit! The rucksack looked familiar, just like the one belonging to the bloody corpse! I shrugged off the idiotic fear that lurked in the back of my mind and we walked, slowly feeling our way with our boots. It was almost impossible to see. It wasn't a companionable walk; he was in front as we stepped down the slippery rough path towards Side Farm. If it hadn't been for the mist, I'd have shot off on my own, scooted off as fast as my legs would take me. The proverbial hair on the back of my neck prickled as we trudged blindly down from Boredale Hause. He looked so like the guy who had taken his own life.

'Do you walk much?' he asked. He half turned and looked over his shoulder at me.

'Yes, I was last on this path a few months ago. Before that, when I did the Coast to Coast, a couple of years ago.'

'Oh when did you do it? What time of year? I did it two years ago too.' The man stopped and smiled.

'Let me see...May/June. I can't quite remember.' I stopped too; I didn't want to take a step nearer.

'Good time of year that. Same as me. It's a wonder we didn't bump into each other.' The man gave a little laugh.

I didn't answer; I nodded – which he didn't see. I was still trying to lag behind, put some distance between us. I was very glad we hadn't bumped into each other and we walked on in silence before he felt the need to speak once more.

'Where else have you been? Have you completed your Wainwright's?' The man trudged steadily on. We hadn't swapped names and I really didn't want to encourage any further exchange, although his voice was interesting, hypnotising and deep, like Shakespearean actors, yet it had a soft, gentle tone that drew me in. Occasionally he looked over his shoulder, checked I was still with him. I didn't want him to look at me again and I pulled my zip up as high as it could go, like it would offer protection.

'I only finished them last year. Great End was my final,' I said through my muffled jacket.

'Great End you say?' From the tone of his voice, I knew he was smiling.

'Yeah!' My voice didn't sound like mine; it was raised, quivery. Girly. The gloom held sound tight to its chest and I knew no one else could hear us. I suddenly felt very vulnerable. I didn't want to hear any more from him. I deepened my voice, adding, 'Great End. Fitting...I thought...'

'Funny that. I finished on Great End last year too.'

It was not funny. It was not funny at all. It was deeply uncomfortable and I halted under the pretext of tying my boot lace hoping he would walk on. He waited. I could just about make out his jacket in the murk. I was thoroughly spooked. My breathing was laboured, my chest tight.

'What month?' he persisted. Mist swirled. It was becoming colder. Much colder.

'It was early. In March. Yeah, March. Yeah.' I wanted him to bugger off.

He laughed, 'It seems we have a lot in common!' The man stopped walking and fixedly stared at me. I didn't like his eyes piercing right through me, slicing through the gloom, slicing through my thoughts. I undid the other boot and made light-hearted comments about needing to sort the other one too. I kept my head down, but he gave a gentle cough, letting me know he was still waiting. He wasn't going to walk without me. He wasn't going anywhere. The only way I was going to get off the fell was to follow. 'I finished in March too,' he said.

I felt sick, I really didn't want to hear about his Wainwright adventures and deliberately lagged more but he knew the game and waited. One after the other, we leapt over a small stream before reaching the Victorian iron bench close to the end of the path. It is a little bit of civilisation in rough terrain. I'm always grateful the bench hasn't been replaced by one from Elizabeth's reign. It isn't far from the road that leads to the pub (boy I needed a drink!) and it attracts its fair share of Sunday strollers who walk no further. If benches could talk, it would tell some tales. Perhaps it would tell mine? Damn it! He sat down and gestured for me to sit beside him. He gave a fleeting look over his shoulder at shrouded Place Fell and we acknowledged there really was a mountain behind us. Slowly, he opened the lid of his rucksack and I realised I was shaking – it wasn't purely dithering from cold! I was afraid but was beyond analysing why. He pulled out a hat, unpinned a 214 badge and handed it to me saying, 'Here, you deserve this.'

'Why? What for?' I was perplexed, yet the brush of his hand was strangely comforting.

'Why not?' He shrugged, 'I keep a few for Completers I meet. The ones who don't register. I don't give them to everyone. My father belonged to the society; it was something he really believed in and I literally follow in his footsteps. He disappeared not long ago. I don't know what happened to him, whether he's dead or alive. I miss him. He's out there somewhere and one day I'll find him.'

Calling Card

'She is yours.' That's all she said to me. Time stretched between us and I felt unable to breathe. I still couldn't when she stepped forward and said, 'Look! She has your eyes.' I do recall the moment of madness when this woman, Petra or whatever her name was, pulled me close, urgently, and I'd followed her down the thin sliver of alley-way, up the steeply turning stone steps to her flat above the shop. It truly was madness and I slipped into the abyss.

I didn't usually go to concerts but Kendal called and the tickets I'd acquired were free. My wife didn't want to go. I can't blame the drink. Or even the drugs. Just madness. And here she was saying this baby was mine. My flesh and blood.

She wore a sling on her front and a small rucksack on her back. Her legs were long and slim, covered in runner's leggings. She still looked fit but more tired and lined than I remembered. The sling was a thin, green material with blotched patches —presumably from baby yuck — and its bump was the only part of her that looked curvy. But this was preposterous. I barged past, ran out of the Information Centre she'd spotted me in and melded into Ambleside's crowded pavements.

******

Three weeks later I caught sight of her, hurrying up the fellside behind me, sling tied round her like a large neckerchief ready to tuck into dinner. I raced on and lost her easily. Yet, she must have been watching, somehow got wind of where I'd be. I'm part of the Park Ranger team and my whereabouts are easy enough to track if you know who to ask. I tried keeping a low profile, but she appeared again a few days later, scurrying up Garburn Pass. I hid behind a rock, took off my jacket and stuffed it in my pack, pulled on a hat and changed direction. I watched her head uphill as I headed down.

Life moved on and I hoped I'd seen the last of Petra but I caught her loitering outside my office a few weeks later. I often went into work early, got there before the roads became filled with tourists. There she was with one of those buggies the athletic types choose. It had wheels that bump over anything allowing the parent to push and run. She had her back to me and was rolling it back and forth; even from my position I could tell she was agitated and no doubt the baby was too. I sat in the car, my indicator ticking to turn right. I turned left and put my foot down.

My phone rang half an hour later and I knew it was the office. 'Hi yeah, change of plan this morning. What? Sorry, Sue, I can't hear. You're breaking up. Bad signal.' I finished the call, looked in my mirror and accelerated. It rang again ten minutes later and I pulled over into a clearing. 'What is it now?' I asked, none too kindly.

'John, I'm sorry to call you again, but there's a woman here insisting she speaks only to you. In fact she's in the foyer and' – Sue giggled nervously – 'she is changing her baby's nappy. But she said she'll wait for you however long it takes.'

'I see.' I didn't. 'Okay. Thanks, Sue.' Wild ideas ripped through my head but I realised I had to deal with this or it wouldn't go away and told Sue to give the woman a coffee and I would be there in half an hour.

******

I couldn't believe I'd got myself into such a mess. Everything was on the line. My wife would never forgive me as it was the one thing I could never give her. Not having family was eating away at Marion and sadly eroding our marriage. I felt unable to get anything right and this wasn't helping. I pulled into a parking slot and through the smoked glass I saw her, stick thin and agitated. I bit the bullet, pulled up my collar and strode into the building.

'It's okay, Sue.' I waved away her concern. Sue was the most efficient person one could hope to meet; it mildly amused me to see her looking perplexed! Across from her desk, our new temp answered the phone and kept her eyes averted; she normally waved or acknowledged me.

I strode past Petra, muttering, 'Follow me.' I dropped my keys and fumbled with the lock. The baby squirmed in its buggy, troubled mewling sounds came from under the black hood as I ushered them through and as soon as the door closed she hissed, 'Don't for one minute question whether you're the father or not! She is yours!'

Petra was taller than I remembered; she glared at me on a level-pegging. She wore a top that emphasised her protruding ribs and I shuddered, I must have had a skin-full. 'The thing is,' — Petra searched for a tissue to wipe her dripping nose — 'the thing is, I want you to be involved, be a father to her. Every child deserves a father.'

She bent down to the child and stuffed a dummy in its mouth; it clearly didn't want it and spat it out, squirming to free itself of the harness that held it in place. It was restless and the whining noise was getting louder.

'Do you need to feed it or something?' I offered, peering towards the canopy.

Petra turned; her eyes were rounder, bigger than I remembered. 'IT has a name! It's a girl!'

'I'm sorry. What is it...her name?' I swallowed hard; I really didn't want to know.

'Arabella. After my mother.' Petra leaned towards the baby and jerked the buggy hard. 'Bella. Bella. Quiet!' Arabella's face scrunched up and reddened, then the little mite let out the loudest bawl. Sue walked past my internal window trying not to look; she must have caught my scowl as she visibly speeded up and scuttled along the corridor. Petra jiggled the buggy again but was losing the battle to halt the howling, hungry child. I didn't know what to do but was saved from offering suggestions when she opened the office door, glared and said she would be back. I had no doubt she would return. I couldn't wait.

******

She was back about a week later and I swear she wore the same clothes but they hung limply, nothing padded them out. She looked a mess. Sue, ever the diplomat, hadn't asked questions the first time but this time she knocked on my door and said, 'There's someone to see you, the woman with the child is in the foyer. Coffee?'

I nodded and sighed, 'Show her through.'

'Arabella's asleep. I left her with the woman on reception. It's a nice place you have. Looks like you have a great set-up here.' Petra nodded and looked around. Her cheekbones were sharper than a week ago. 'Have you thought about her? Have you thought about me? Us? Our life together?' Petra's chin jutted upwards, a defiance in her stance. 'I need to know when we'll be together.'

She went through a pretence of looking at my certificates on the wall but I knew she was using the glass reflection to gauge me, weigh me up. She whirled round and stared, tilted her head to the side. 'I knew you were the right one, the fact that we were both Environmental Scientists. Fancy that! I knew Bella would have good genes. Me with my Doctorate and you with yours in..? I can't remember. Go on. Remind me.'

She tilted her head further and the pupils of her eyes shrank as she looked towards the window. 'You'll make a great dad,' she said almost to herself. 'I know you will.'

After a moment of staring out of the Velux and me trying to assess her, she dashed off saying she would be back. Of that, I had no doubt.

Sue knocked lightly, opened my door slower than she would normally. She peered over her glasses at me and asked, 'I know it's none of my business but.... your friend, is she okay?' I held back, said nothing. 'She's very, erm, thin isn't she?' Sue took her cue from my stony features and left the room.

******

Some time passed and I did wonder about the baby. It had a sweet face and looked a bit like my youngest brother, I mused as I walked to Greggs for a pasty. Later that morning I caught sight of her pushing the buggy, trotting along by the Salutation. She looked like she would snap in two and I stopped and watched as she turned the corner. It was the last time I saw her.

I carried on walking; I admit I was curious as to where she lived and I hurried along trying to catch another glimpse of her and Bella. I thought I saw her by Bridge House, the tiny National Trust building, and thought she might just fit it with her minute frame. But it wasn't her, she'd gone. It was early and I walked and walked and found myself doing the whole of the Fairfield round. I would mention the baby to Marion soon. I had clarity. Walking did that for me. Cleared my brain. I would mention my baby. Soon.

******

Any hope of gently easing Marion into the situation was wrenched from my hands the following day when Social Services rang. Sue took the call and it was that look over her glasses which told me to expect trouble.

'Mr Talbot?' The voice was bland; I deduced nothing other than that the person calling was female. I suspected I was in for a hard time. I was required to go in and see them.

******

'Marion, sit down.'

'I will in a minute, I'm just going to finish off these spuds.' Marion picked up an oven glove, put it down again and rubbed the small of her back. 'I bloody hate cooking!'

'Well why are you faffing around tonight? We could have picked up a takeaway or gone out for a bite to eat.' I offered.

'Oh, I dunno. I suppose I wanted to do something healthy. We had a takeaway a few days ago. I haven't got time for all this shopping and chopping.' Marion pressed her lips together before hitting the microwave button six times and it chugged along, waltzing away a dizzying portion of cauliflower. Cooking was not Marion's forte. I opened a bottle of white and passed her a glass, biding my time.

'What was your day like?' I asked.

'Rather like yesterday. If Johnston thinks I'm going to go, he's got another think coming!' Marion was in battle mode.

I took another slug of wine. 'Well, perhaps it is time you moved on...'

Marion threw the oven glove at me, red rags and bulls. 'Why the fuck should I?' she snorted. 'I've given them twelve years of graft, twelve years when I could have been doing something else. I've given them my best, John! And look where it's got me! Look where it's got us! It's all too bloody late!' She stomped off muttering about IVF. It was all about to hit the fan.

I took another slug and waited until after dinner before saying anything more.

'Sorry about the potatoes, I think they needed a bit longer. Sorry I was grumpy. I've had it up to here with work.'

'It doesn't matter.' I coughed. 'Marion?'

'What? You looked very serious for a moment then. I thought you were going to say something pithy.' She giggled and took a slug herself.

'I do have something to say and it's not going to be easy.'

******

Marion walked out. I was on my own for the first time in years and I walked in to Social Services the following day. It transpired that Petra was unable to look after the child. She had been hospitalised and the baby had been taken into care. I was named as the father and would I be prepared to look after Arabella? It was all too fast. Too sudden. But there was the copy of the birth certificate and my name was on it.

'As the father, keeping the child within the family is important. We can discuss help that you may require as we go along.' The woman opposite me was young; she looked about seventeen, earnest and well-meaning like she had a lifetime of social work ahead of her. I hoped she wouldn't burn-out too quickly. I squirmed in my seat and considered putting up an opposing viewpoint, but I said nothing, other than I would consider it before I made my way out into the fresh air. I bought a packet of cigarettes and smoked three – one after another – something I hadn't done in twelve years. I felt sick. I crumpled the box and threw it in the nearest bin.

******

Arabella changed my life. She came home with me a little while later. I knew nothing, except something in this child gave me hope, a hope for the future I hadn't experienced before. I felt different, like a new adventure stretched ahead of me. I had no idea how it would turn out. I found myself really excited and took time off work to get to know my daughter.

Marion moved house, my betrayal being too much. I never saw her again. My cruelty would live with me forever. Some months later I did the DNA test that was offered. The result didn't surprise me. It didn't matter she wasn't of my flesh. I had bonded with my little one and life would never be the same again.

Devotion

He had to do it. Had to. It was who he was. No one would understand just how much pleasure it gave him. No psychiatrist. No doctor. Not even his mother. The satisfaction was immense. The watching. The stalking. The waiting and finally, the grab!

He particularly liked young, pretty women and if they had long dark hair the better. Somehow they put up the most fight and didn't resort to tears – which never worked anyway, it always hardened him further.

He could sleep soundly in his bed at night. These women put themselves in the wrong position in the first place, he reasoned. A little more care, a little more thought and they wouldn't find themselves in such a vulnerable situation.

At the end of the day, Jonathon went home to his mother. They lived together in a three-storey house in Keswick close to the park. His mother was bent double now, riddled with arthritis and on every anti-inflammatory known to man. She lived on the bottom floor which was specially adapted to suit her needs. He had made most of the changes himself, even putting an extra toilet in under the stairs. He was proud of that as his plumbing skills had been learned via the internet. His next job was to change the handles on all the doors. Knobs were out, handles were in.

'What are you looking at?' his mother shuffled down the hall, resting against her walker. 'You looked very serious there, son.' She struggled to raise her head.

'Oh I was just looking at ways of taking these off.' He pointed at the knobs and scratched his head with a pencil. 'I might need to buy an electric screwdriver. It would come in handy for all sorts of things.' Jonathon stayed on his knees and looked up at his mother with the cauliflower hair-do.

'Son, don't worry about those, I can manage, I don't bother closing doors anymore. You have enough to think about in that demanding job of yours.'

Jonathon got up and smiled at his white-haired, shrunken mother and almost patted her on the head except she hated her hair messed up so he stopped just short. 'Do you want me to help you get into bed yet?'

'No! I can manage, I'm all right tonight. Some nights I'm creakier than others but tonight is all right.' He watched her toddle off, her bingo perm jiggling with each placement of the frame.

Jonathon did tuck her up. He made her a cup of warm milk, put it on her bedside table and propped her up with four pillows which held her firmly upright. He turned his attention to her feet and shuffled a frame into place before pulling blankets over it.

'There, how's that? Feet okay? No pressure?'

'Can you just pull that cover down? It looks untidy all scrunched up like that.'

'Here?'

'No. A bit more. That's it. You know what I'm like.' Jonathon knew all right. The conversation in their home was the same every night. But he loved his mother and he was happy when she was happy. He could forgive her anything.

'Okay. Here's your milk. A pale blue straw for you tonight – to match your nightie.'

Jonathon and his mother chuckled before she took a suck and she wiped her dribble on his crumpled handkerchief. He fetched the hairspray and she put her hands over her mouth and eyes as he sprayed and sprayed before fixing her hairnet in place. When she deemed it dry enough to lie down, he helped ease her under her eiderdown and smoothed the top of the striped flannelette sheet into place.

'There, all done!' He patted it and watched as a withered hand struggled to hold a battered copy of 'Rescue Me My Love' by Rosy Banks. He rolled his eyes. He wished someone would rescue him. One page a night was all she could manage. Still, if it kept her entertained...thank goodness he didn't have to buy them from the shop anymore. That was just too much! He drew the line at some things and his mother's reading choice was vastly different from his. Most of which he kept hidden, but now she couldn't take the stairs, he could leave anything lying around.

He sat and waited until her mouth dropped open and she snored before getting up to make himself a decaf. As far as he knew, she slept through the night without waking as he never heard a sound, but he wondered whether he would hear if she called out as his room was on the top floor. He decided a baby monitor might be a good idea but he wasn't in the mood to seek one out tonight. He had other stuff on his mind, like checking the webcams he had access to. It had been a long day. After ten minutes he returned, peeped in, made sure Mum was still sleeping soundly and spent a couple of hours on the internet. He trawled and trolled, shouted at the screen and vowed he'd find another.

******

And he did – the very next day. He picked her out easily, watched her from his vantage point – being the girth of a large oak tree. He watched her drive and park up. But she changed her mind and drove off. He walked all around town – three times – but had no luck and resigned himself to going home to Mother.

Mother wasn't good; she was in a lot of pain and when an extra couple of tablets had no affect, he bundled her into their Berlingo and set off for Penrith. He trundled along the A66 hitting rush-hour traffic. It was bad. He hated traffic.

The Walk-In Centre was strangely quiet and they hoped they wouldn't have to wait long before being seen. They sat on plastic chairs and talked about his day. His mother prodded and poked him in the ribs and theatrically whispered, 'That young girl is pretty. Just like your sister was.' Jonathon ignored her initially, but when she persisted with the conversation, he said he was going to find a machine for a bottle of water and left her sitting alone. He preferred not to think about his deceased big sister - since everything fell on his shoulders.

When he returned, she was in with the 'pretty one' and Mother was on her best behaviour nodding and saying, 'Yes, yes, yes,' even though he knew she wasn't taking anything in and it would all have to be repeated for his sake. It turned out to be a bad case of indigestion and Mother could not contain her wind any longer. Along the A66 and in the shadow of Blencathra, he suffered in silence as Mother broke loose and free and he wound the window down a touch hoping she wouldn't notice. She did, but looked the other way.

******

The following day was long and hot and he loosened the neck of his shirt as he returned home. The whole day had gone badly from start to finish and it got a whole lot worse when he saw the stack of envelopes sitting in the wire cage behind the door. He'd spotted the white envelope and the council frank mark.

His mother called through, 'I've made your favourite!' He didn't have the heart to tell her he no longer liked cottage pie. He last enjoyed it about five years ago but it was on the table approximately every ten days. His mother struggled in the kitchen now but this was one thing she felt she could still do for her son. So he ate the grey mess with hard lumps of mashed potatoes, made appropriate appreciative noises and scraped his plate clean. Every time.

'What's the letter?' His mother couldn't miss the envelope propped up before him.

'It looks like rubbish.'

'Aren't you going to open it then?' His mother hovered close with a tea-towel draped over her shoulder.

'I'll read it later. It's probably junk mail.' He shoved it in his back pocket and his mother blinked rapidly before shuffling to the sink. She began to sing and whilst she had her back turned he opened it. He was requested to go into the office the next day. He laughed aloud, over-jolly, and said, 'Oh it's only some rubbish. Nothing to worry about, Mother.'

******

'Over-zealous! Over-zealous? How the heck can you be over-zealous? You either do the job or you don't? I don't get it Bob. I really don't.' Jonathon looked at his colleague of over thirty years.

'Look Jonathon, there have been complaints. Many. Your name comes up time after time and you are on a warning. That's all I'm saying. You are on a warning.' Bob shrugged, shuffled papers and no longer looked at his colleague.

Jonathon returned to work and thought very carefully about what had been said, but later in the day he saw her. He couldn't help it. Just one more. She was the sort he liked and when the long-haired lass was late returning to her car, he barely contained his whoop, his joy. At the very last second, he slapped a parking ticket right where you couldn't miss it — and then went home to Mother.

Dismissed

Queen of the Lakes sailed on time for her last trip of the day. She docked and disgorged her passengers in the small northern village of Pooley Bridge. The village thrived because of the boats. They thrived because people enjoyed the glamour. This was Doreen's opinion. Oh yes, the boats were glamorous; they hinted of times past when life was not so busy, not so hurried. They had a faded elegance that warmed her heart as they sailed from one end of the lake to the other.

Doreen had always wanted to steer a boat. A proper boat, not something hired and handed back at the end of an hour — it had to be a big one. And when her chance came to enter a competition, she was beside herself with excitement, she would enter it without telling a soul. 'Steer it like a pro' the sign said and it whetted her whistle no end. Five tickets (as proof she had used the service) were needed to support her entry and umpteen pages of kitchen notepad were used before she found her winning line.

'I want to skipper an Ullswater steamer because...'

Doreen was dismissed. Dismissed by her family when she wanted to learn to drive. They didn't think she had enough *spacial awareness* and so she never did.

Doreen was dismissed. She wanted to teach. Once. But no one thought she could do it and raise a family at the same time. *Too many buses to catch. Getting to college would be difficult, especially in winter.* It seemed there were too many reasons for not doing what she desired.

Doreen was dismissed. Many years ago she was dismissed for stealing. Except it wasn't her fault. She didn't take the coat; she just had one of those faces that blushed when questioned.

Doreen's father had worked on boats, yet her family dismissed her desire to be close to them. Dismissed her desire to seek them out, to see their brightly painted hulls and marvel at their wind-ripped flags. She wanted to touch varnished rails and trail her fingers along faded ropes. She needed a connection to her past and hope for her future.

Doreen had left the others to walk on Barton Fell; she said she wanted to take the steamer and would meet them at Howtown when the boat docked. She wanted some time to think. She wriggled out of her tiny rucksack and sat with her back against the scarlet funnel. Out of the breeze, it would be the best place to sit. She knew the boat would reverse, turn around to sail and her hair would not be in her face. She knew how it worked. Today was bright and hazy; she tilted her face to the cool March sun and shut her eyes. She smiled at the familiar crackle of the safety message having heard it so many times before and glanced around knowing few could understand what the recording actually said. She looked at her ticket and beamed; this was her passage to success, number five: she would post it today.

Earlier in the week, she had sat in the kitchen at her tiny Formica table and thought about winning. 'I want to skipper an Ullswater Steamer because...' The line hung with nothing to attach to it. 'I want to skipper an Ullswater Steamer because...I just do!' Doreen shouted and threw her last piece of shopping list paper in the direction of the sink. She snorted as it missed and fell to the floor. She scribbled once more on the inside of a packet of PG.

'Is that you Doreen love? What's the matter? Put the kettle on will you, and make us a brew?' Doreen decided to ignore Harold. She would make one later when Heartbeat had finished. He liked Heartbeat.

'Because, because, because...'

******

She pressed her back into the warm metal; against the funnel was the warmest place to be when it was cold. Her ticket was a winner. Somehow she knew it. Inspiration had come at last! She just had to make sure she caught the post and the prize would be hers. She glanced at the wheelhouse and watched someone run up the wooden steps and shout to the skipper, but she couldn't hear what was said. It was all so exciting. Did all skippers wear hats at jaunty angles? Doreen thought they must. She would be up there, she knew she would.

The waters boiled as the boat reversed and Doreen sat contained, serene and delighted. These were her stolen moments, moments that stilled her deep inside. The more the water churned, the calmer she felt. At one. At home. Try getting the family to understand that.

And when her ticket won, her family understood none of it.

'What do you want to do that for?' her daughter asked.

'What made you enter that?' said Harold, but Doreen hugged the letter tight to her chest and walked away with her head held high. The prize was hers.

******

The winning day dawned but she was determined not to be flustered. 'That's it Maureen, just turn your face this way a bit more.' Doreen turned to the camera and held tight. She glanced back at the highly glossed wood with its gleaming brass knowing she didn't want to leave finger-marks. She couldn't see a way of steering without doing so and wiped it with the sleeve of her anorak before beaming for the camera once more. She caught her reflection in the brass, thought she looked long in the tooth, but it wasn't the time to care.

When the photographs were done, the skipper took her elbow and pointed out various dials. He told her what to focus on and not to be nervous; someone would be with her all the time, although *she* was skipper for the evening. They would be on their way soon. For a brief moment before the engine started, she was left alone and looked over her shoulder down at the deck towards her bemused family who were standing awkwardly holding their glasses of fizz. One of the boat's assistants said something to them and they nodded and sat. She waved to them but no one noticed. She took a deep breath and gripped the wheel. It felt solid, it felt right and soon they were steaming down the lake.

By the time The Queen had reached the centre, Doreen was standing tall, her feet planted firmly a foot apart. She was glad she'd bought new yachting shoes. The mountains all around enfolded her, hugged her. This was where she was meant to be. Harold tapped the window and he was ushered in.

'Isn't your wife doing marvellously?' he was asked, but Doreen didn't hear his reply. Somehow it didn't matter. With her chin thrust upwards, she beamed until it hurt.

At Glenridding there were more photo requests and people shook her hand. She didn't know who they were but thought they must be important. Everyone seemed to be looking her way. Her hand was pumped and the cameras flashed, her face ached from smiling. She was handed a cap with a logo and sheepishly put it on backwards like the Deck Hand who passed it her. Folk were laughing with her, not at her for a change. Her family, now on the pier, kicked their feet and muttered. She could tell from their rounded shoulders they had had enough, but someone was about to speak and they all looked up.

'And so ladies and gentlemen, I give you our winner, Doreen Murdock, for her winning line...' the man handed the microphone to her and she said something. No one heard. She needed to hold it closer. The man smiled, pulled a silly face at the crowd and pushed it near her nose. Doreen faltered, coughed and said, 'Erm...' the microphone squealed. The man spoke again.

'Doreen your winning line? ... "I want to skipper an Ullswater Steamer because..."'

Doreen stood proud; felt herself getting taller and said, 'I want to skipper an Ullswater Steamer because — one day my boat will come in!'

Egg On My Face

Don't put them all in one basket. That's what Mum always advised when I was a kid. But what do you do when you need a different kind of advice? The sort of advice when you're cragfast? I can't go up and I can't go down. I see no basket to put my eggs in. I am stuck on a rock, on a mountain, in The Lakes.

The day started off normally enough with my boyfriend and me getting out of the right side of the bed together — there was no left — it being pinned up against the wall. The Ambleside Bed and Breakfast was a little on the small side to say the least but it wasn't expensive and we were on a tight budget. I'd eaten scrambled eggs this morning. Oh the irony! Scrambling the rock face was fun at first. Of course I didn't plan on spending hours alone watching the birds fly past. I wondered how many eggs were in a Crow's clutch? I was making a right oeuf of myself. Mild hysteria was clearly setting in. I was giggling aloud at my jokes.

I found myself on a ledge, a grassy flat bit, roughly six feet square, but I couldn't see a way up. Unfortunately for me, I couldn't see a way down.

It was high summer and if you have to get stuck on a fell, I had, at least, got the time of year right. The views to the south were extensive and I was resigned to sitting it out. I had plenty of food and drink and Harry would look for me soon. We'd separated because he wanted to seek out a particular waterfall, walk up it and in it. I didn't. We agreed to meet on Pavey Ark summit. He would wait there.

I must have dozed off in the sunshine, a dark shadow from the overhang made my special little place rather cold. I studied the rocky route once more. The way I'd come up was slippery, just too dangerous for descent and as for going upwards — I couldn't extend my reach enough to grasp any handhold. I was stuffed. It was not the best situation to be in. There was nothing for it but to call Mountain Rescue.

'Bollocks!' I realised Harry had my phone and I'd gone off piste. No one was going to come this way. I yelled and heard nothing but the return of a Herdy bleat. Nothing but the caw of a bird. I yelled again, somewhat louder and the sheep bleated back. I did have my whistle but my appetite wasn't whetted — yet. I knew I was a plonker of the first order and the embarrassment factor was huge. I actually knew some of the people involved in local mountain rescue so I decided to try and move again. I turned on to my stomach and inched backwards over the edge. I couldn't feel anything with my feet, panicked and pulled myself up. I knew I needed another try and it had to be on my stomach as my rucksack would snag otherwise. I slithered backwards. My feet dangled and I squirmed a bit more, wriggled my feet. I was desperate for rock contact. Tapped to the left. Tapped to the right. Tapped nothing. It was no good; I had to pull myself back up. But I couldn't. There was nothing to push against. My blood ran cold. I gripped hard, clung to wet holds. My face was stuffed with bits of grass. I could hold no longer. My fingers were slipping. Sliding. My breathing was the fastest ever, my heart rate pounded in my ears. I was going to vomit, faint. I clutched at bits of grass which were slipping through my fingers. I was on the precipice. My stomach somersaulted. Then it happened. My body went over. I think I flew.

******

Had I died and gone to heaven? I was all over the place. I remember the sky behind two faces was the bluest of blue and the hair on their heads shone bright and gold like haloes. They were beautiful but I couldn't understand a word they said, yet I was entranced by the smaller 'celestial beings' that flitted around them. Rainbow colours dazzled and I felt good. I smiled at the little ones and they smiled back. They waved and reminded me of Tinkerbell and I laughed. My mother would say I was in 'La La Land'...but it was such a lovely place to be.

'No wait! Don't go!' I urged the little sparkly ones to stay as they danced and dashed — clearly on their way somewhere and I began to hear ugly sounds and the harsh light of reality disturbed my happy world. A bright light shone in my eyes and my lids were prised open by insistent fingers. I recoiled.

'Hello there. You've had a nasty fall. Hello?'

I shut my eyes again; the fluttery little people were only just about there, translucent and waving over their shoulders. Their sad little faces broke my heart. 'Hello there. That's better. Hi, I'm Dr. Martin. Susan Martin. Can you remember your name?'

Of course I could. It took a moment though, the little beings called me 'Star' and I rather liked that. I closed my eyes again. Their tinkling voices were receding, they were flying away. They'd gone. The voice made them go. I was catapulted out of my Lilliput world.

'Hello? Open your eyes, please. Look at me. Hello again. You are with me now. Good. Can you tell me your name?'

'Angie,' I managed to croak.

'Ah, one of the angels hey?' the doctor smiled.

'You could say that.' It hurt to talk. I was so tired.

'You were out walking. Did you have anyone with you?'

Remembering Harry was easy, but the two beautiful faces flashed through my mind and I uttered a cry.

'Are you okay? We've given you a sedative, you have some cracked ribs and we've bound up your wrist. You have some serious bruising. You were lucky it wasn't much worse. You fell quite a way. You must have bounced. Luck was on your side — you'll live!' Dr. Martin said kindly as she touched my hand.

'The faces? The blonde people? I couldn't understand what they said...' I was drifting into La La Land once more when Dr. Martin's voice cut through, 'Yes, you were found by a lovely couple. You were lucky. Apparently they were on holiday from Sweden and wandered off track. No wonder you couldn't understand them!'

Food For Thought

Stuart chose Keswick after a chance stop-over but wouldn't admit to anyone he fell in love with Skiddaw's backdrop and thought the English Lake District the most beautiful place in Britain. No self-respecting Scot would admit to that. Not outwardly anyway.

The mountain was certainly enticing, but he was used to bigger ones and never failed to tell anyone who would take the time to listen. It was all a bit of fun. Munroes were more his thing. It's not that he deliberately set out to wind people up, it was just that he couldn't resist having a poke — usually at other people's expense. Munroes were the mahoosive ones. The real McCoy where real walkers went. Coupled with his Glaswegian accent, he expected Keswick wouldn't take to him immediately. And he was right. Business was slow.

Stuart had been warned the food business was fickle and setting up a fish bar when there were at least two others was, at best, foolhardy. But he would not be told. He needed to make this work. It was all he knew. His dad had a fish shop before him and his grandfather before him worked in a fish market. And great grandfather was a fisherman who was out on the seas in all weather! Fish was his business. Fish was in his blood. But his older brother had inherited the lot.

'It's okay. I needed the fresh start. I'll make them love me,' he was fond of saying.

'How?' questioned the voice on the other end of the phone.

'Och, I'll just batter 'em!' was the familiar and flippant reply and Stuart laughed until he coughed.

'A rheumy cough and food don't go together, Stuart. You'll have to give up the fags. The big 4-0 isn't far off.' His little sister Margaret was always looking out for him. 'Go and do more of those fells you keep talking about.'

'Aye, you're right, hen. Got to go. A customer... and I need as many as I can get.' He switched off his mobile and put it on the shelf where he could see it.

He wiped his hands on his apron and chucked the greasy chip basket into the boiling fat. He called over his shoulder, 'Are ye for a fish supper?' He smiled at himself and tried again, 'Fish and chips? Mine are the best, ye know.' He couldn't help wink at the woman who had entered his shop. She was bearing a rucksack which was at least half her height and she emptied the entire contents onto the low window-ledge. He carried on shuffling chips and watched in the mirror. He assessed she was about thirty-five, slim and fit and didn't eat chips that often. Shame.

'Have ye had a good walk?' He nodded at the bag.

'Yes, thanks.' The woman bent over her rucksack, rifled through every pocket until she found her money. 'Thank God I found my purse; I'm starving! Yeah, I did the Coledale round. It was brilliant! It's a bit cold now and I just fancied some chips. I need something hot inside me. It's freezing out there.'

'I have nae done that one yet,' he laughed. 'In fact, I have nae done any.' He had, in fact, done most of them.

The woman smiled and shrugged, not sure whether to nod or shake her head; she could barely understand his accent.

'Och, sorry lass.' He wiped his hands once more and tried speaking with less of an accent. 'Coledale? Is-that-another-of-those-Wainwright-bloke-walks?' he said, pronouncing every syllable. He knew he shouldn't be disparaging. He knew all about Wainwright but wasn't going to crack-on to this wee woman — or anyone else who cared to stroll through the door. It was more fun to pretend. More fun to wind the English up.

He failed to notice she was trying hard not to laugh and he was so taken by the twinkle in her eye he burnt his finger on the counter but he did notice she was biting her lip.

She composed herself, 'Yes, it is — and one worth doing if you are bagging all 214. You can tick quite a few off on that route. I did it last year but the weather was foul and I promised myself I'd come back and do it on a better day. See the views. They are pretty spectacular.'

'Salt and vinegar?' he paused, held the vinegar bottle in mid-air, knowing the three little words had blended into one and probably sounded like 'sovinger'. 'Salt-and-vinegar?' he repeated with exaggerated slowness and this time couldn't fail to notice her struggle to keep her face straight; the poor girl was nodding with great enthusiasm.

Stuart wrapped once, twice and handed the packet over. He muttered something about needing a Wainwright education.

The woman responded with a jolly, 'You do. See you!' and walked out.

It was half an hour before anyone else came in for a fish supper.

A man and woman struggled to enter The Keswick Frier. Rucksack clips clashed and strained before pulling apart. Stuart acknowledged them but they only grunted and tilted their heads towards the price list behind him. He wondered if they were foreign? They looked like students. He tuned in for an accent as they began a discussion, but their voices were low, yet hard and he wasn't privy to their innermost thoughts on the merits of sausage versus meat pie. Their demeanour suggested lovers who weren't so fond of each other that day. Perhaps they'd had a row? A bit of hot fish would do them good. They counted money between them and he carried on turning, churning chips, shook and banged them in their wire basket two times and expertly flipped them into a waiting, warming pan. He picked crumbs off the counter and stirred bright green mushy peas. Steam rose. The couple were still counting pennies. He lifted the metal lid off the curry and stirred it round and round. He might add sultanas. That would be exotic. Stuart wiped the counter, turned the cloth and rubbed at a mark on the mirror. He wouldn't normally have such patience. Finally, they ordered.

'One fishcake and small chips please.'

Oh joy! Rolls Royce next week! He was saved from his sarcasm breaking free when the woman bent down and exclaimed, 'Oh, there's an earring here! What a shame someone lost it — is good one!' Her accent was Eastern European he decided. Confirmed by the cheekbones. Educated though. Probably Daddy had a castle in Transylvania. His thoughts did amuse him. Something had to. Life was too dull. More chip-chompers were needed.

Stuart held out his hand. He knew exactly who it belonged to. He gave the couple extra chips and said, 'Ta-ta!'

It was the wee lassie's; it must have fallen out when she pulled off her bonnet.

He looked at the small pearl earring and was reminded of the famous painting. His pretty customer had short dark hair and was nothing like Vermeer's beauty. The girl with the pearl earring. Of course! Here was another fish connection! Pearls come from shells! It all comes down to fish! He banged his fist on the hot counter. It always came down to fish! She may not look anything like the painting but he was happy with the tenuous connection. He kissed the little orb and gently placed it on the shelf where he could keep an eye on it. She would be back. He knew it and tossed more chips in the air.

High Spirits

It was a dark and stormy night and I could barely see into the back yard as I stood trying to remember who wrote the famous line. I scratched the back of my head and tried to think who came up with it first? I snorted on remembering Snoopy nicked it a few times but generally I didn't have a clue. I watched the moon appear and disappear but for the main part there was nothing to see. It was Quink — as my grandmother used to say. I occasionally caught a glimpse of the fells; those dark forbidding humps that would take on a different hue in daylight. I was looking forward to my planned walk up High Pike and on to Carrock the following day. I walked into the kitchen; the window was well steamed up. I wiped the condensation with my sleeve and peered through once more — why I looked a second time, I don't know but there was plenty of noise going on. It really was a dark and stormy night. I slopped back into the lounge and fell into a comfy chair until I heard a noise in the kitchen and remembered.

The toast! I'd left it on the grill and raced to find flames leaping up the front of the ancient cooker. I blew and blew on the burnt offering but my simple supper was burnt to a crisp and now the smoke detector was deciding to have a dicky fit! I grabbed a tea-towel and wafted for Britain. I put the last of the bread on the blackened grill-pan and while I hovered over it, I Googled the infamous opening line. Hmm? A guy called Edward Bulwer-Lytton penned it for a novel written in 1830. It did not get rave reviews. I munched my toast as I looked at my phone. It seemed I shared his first name but that was probably all we had in common. Perhaps he wrote the line on a night like tonight? The kettle boiled and clicked off. I couldn't remember flicking the switch to on — but made coffee anyway.

Something crashed outside. There was a great deal of *whatever* being flung around. There was nothing for it but to go to bed early and have a read. I could put earplugs in. I'd brought some knowing I'd be sharing the place for two nights, but I didn't expect I'd need them when I was alone! The hostel had dodgy WiFi. I would have to resort to reading a book. There were plenty left lying around. I'd been warned the electricity could go off at any time and on cue the lights dimmed, came on bright for a moment then dimmed once more before I was finally enveloped by darkness. Great. Just great. I sat without moving. I wasn't easily scared and there was a bit of moonlight filtering through so with my phone to hand I had enough light to find my way up the stairs and along the 'spooky corridor' to the dormitory.

It was dubbed 'the spooky corridor' by the guys last night. The girls swore they had picked up 'an atmosphere' and avoided the end of the corridor at all costs. They said it was colder. What a load of rubbish! I had a bit of fun with the guys trying to pull them towards the rooms; I got into trouble for making someone's jumper sleeve longer than the other and my ears took a battering from their screams. It was a great night last night and I did get thumped. It's a good job there are no neighbours as we made enough noise to raise the dead. Maybe that is not the right phrase to use considering. I chuckled. The girls would love me for that.

The hostel is empty now except for me and sixty empty beer cans and not far off the same number of wine bottles! Never again. I laughed: we always say that after a 'good sesh'! I was chuffed to bits Pauline let me stay on an extra night and told me where I could hide the key the following day. A walk on my own would be ace. Pauline, you're a good 'un. I'll buy you some choccies.

I shivered. The girls were right – it was colder down this end of the corridor, but I had noticed cracks in the building and plenty of fresh air managed to whistle into the bathrooms. The gents' was freezing! I wondered if the girls' loos fared any better? I needed the bog before I went to bed; I'd finished off the last of the beer and didn't want to get up in the night. All I had was the light from my phone which was pretty eerie. I pulled a face at myself in the mirror, I looked scary and I decided not to do that again. As I went to leave, the stupid door jammed. It wouldn't budge. I tugged again. My heart rate upped. I pulled and pulled but it took quite an effort to free it. Stupid swollen wood. Further along the corridor a door banged. Draughty old place!

I made my way down that long corridor, felt my way most of the time as the moon had disappeared again. I needed to conserve my phone battery if the power was going to be off all night. Damn! It was pitch. Now was not the time to remember the story of The White Lady. Why was it always a white lady? Not green or pink? Or neon? Mind you a neon apparition right now would be pretty scary. Any apparition would be pretty scary. I'll speak to those girls when I get a chance — filling my head with rubbish! Hand over hand, I felt my way along using the window ledge and was startled when my fingers dipped in something slimy. The stench was disgusting and I wiped my hand on the wall.

I had the same problem with the next door. My exit route was locked. I was sure it was open earlier. I tried to quell the rising fear. Urged myself to think. Get a grip. There had to be logic! And then the penny dropped. The guys had returned to freak me out! Decided it would be great fun to sneak back! We certainly talked enough about ghosts last night. It had to be! I laughed out loud when I put two and two together. I'd find the buggers and turn the tables. I'll bet they tripped the lights. The fuse box is in the hall. I decided to leave the lights off for the moment and I began to breathe normally again before creeping into one of the bedrooms. I'd show them. I'd turn the tables. I reached out and slipped a spare duvet from one of the bunks and draped it around my head and shoulders. A blue patterned lady would have to do. I'd scare the crap out of them.

I tip-toed back along the corridor and stopped when the floorboards creaked. I held my breath, counted to twenty before setting off again. I was certainly warmer with the duvet wrapped around me. I tried the latch and this time the door opened easily, I smiled when it creaked just like in the movies. I paused and considered whether I should hide and wait for them to come back? Or should I creep up on them once I knew where they were? I nipped past the window and glanced out — I could just about see my car but no others. Clever sods had probably parked up the road. I listened for any sound and thought I heard low chatter. They were good. It was like whispers of children and I tip-toed in their direction. I edged nearer to where I thought the sound had come from and threw open the cupboard door. Gotcha!

No. I hadn't. I flicked my phone on and all I saw was a Dyson and some bags of logs and kindling. I could have sworn they were in there. I stopped and listened some more. Ah...they were further away than I thought. Perhaps twenty feet. I heard a faint noise like singing, but it was echoey and sad and I wondered how the hell they managed to sound like that? I shook my head. Ten out of ten guys. Just wait 'til I get to you. You won't be singing — you'll be crying for your mummy, your daddy and your granny when I've finished with you!

I followed softly, stopping every few feet to listen. It was cat and mouse now and I inched up the second staircase, along the corridor and back to where I'd come from. It all looped round. Someone was running a bath! What? In the dark? A lock snapped shut. A bolt rammed into place. I spun round. I knew right then it wasn't my friends.

The hairs on every inch of my body pricked as they moved one by one, sensing the presence of something and rising to the occasion. Something or someone? My breathing was thick and fast and I almost wet myself in terror when a soft whisper of breath barely brushed against my neck. I felt something breathing! I swore fifty filthy expletives and made to run; instead I became tangled by my own two feet and landed on my back. I lashed out, kicked and kicked and screamed like the girls the previous night. From the far end of the corridor something struggled to appear — like it didn't have enough energy to materialise. Whatever it was, was edging closer but I was unable to make my legs work. Unable to get up. My arms flailed as I swore the vilest things I could think of to make it go away. Yet it floated towards me like a photo negative, like a gentle cloud and I screamed as it passed through me.

I heard a click. And was that laughter?

Patterdale Antiques

My farmhouse, Hartside, is too ramshackle and dilapidated for me to do anything with any more. It could do with re-wiring, a better bathroom, the kitchen replacing and half a dozen other things that would make life easier now I'm getting on a bit. It's all down to money. Mind you, it usually is. It is situated in Patterdale, within sight of Boredale Hause and is on the famous C2C — that's the coast to coast for the uninitiated and it's over 350 years old. You may know it. It's been in the family since — oh I don't know when! And now it's in a right sorry state. My son, Michael, moved back in two years ago — along with his wife (one of those who won't lift a finger in case she breaks a nail). How he copes with her attitude I don't know, but he changed after the short stint away from farming life, went all posh and up-market. She's from London. Of all places! Why he couldn't settle with a local girl, I don't know. He seems happy enough — but she's unsettled. Not happy. Her sort never are. Always wanting this. Always wanting that. They've talked of family, but it doesn't include me. Patterdale would welcome the patter of tiny feet. Perhaps they're waiting for me to die? I certainly get the feeling I'm in the way. In my own home! The cheek of it! One thing I've managed to hang on to is the insurance. Michael will eventually get it and doesn't she know it! She – being Federika. What sort of a name is that! Puffed up if you ask me.

I must feed the chickens. It's too early for the stream of tourist cars, but I can see a few walkers heading up Boredale. The valley is quiet and still — except for Flemming's dog. 'Flaming Dog' more like! It never shuts up! It will soon be time to open the barn. Ha! Ahead of the rush. I wish. Thank goodness I have the l'al distraction though. Gives me the space I need. Trust Federika to seize on the idea when I first came up with it. Snotty cow. 'Oh, you could make a fortune, Margaret! All those tourists passing along the road. It's the perfect spot! We must do it!'

The 'spot' down the road, by ten minutes, is my little business. I've only just opened really. It's a bit basic. I sell antiques. I began with shifting a few things from the house, a few unloved vases and such things, a brass plate here, a copper kettle there. I managed to pull out some of the old ploughs and wheels that were left lying around, rubbed them down with coarse sandpaper (that caused a few blisters I can tell you) and I painted them with Hammerite. Mind you, it was the unpainted ones that sold first. Folk can be funny.

The barn is 40' by 20'-ish give or take a foot or two. Michael got a friend to put in a stud wall at the back. There was already water so putting in a bit of a kitchen where I could make tea wasn't too difficult. The problem comes when I need the loo. I have to shut shop, put a note on the door and scuttle off home. I always think that's when someone is going to call in. I only ever get a quick pee.

I've got a lady coming in later today; I'll have to go to the loo early. She rang about some books. I don't want too many of them. They don't sell. You sometimes get Dealers coming in. I don't like them, rifling through things in that manner of theirs, thinking you are too thick to understand or too deaf to hear. I always tell them I can hear very well thank you.

Federika and Michael are shouting at each other. I wish they'd shut their bloody window. They're always at it. I'm going to bang on the back door. That'll shut them up. Oh to be free of the pair of them. I wish I had the house to myself. Michael has already suggested a little flat. I told him what he could do with his little suggestion.

******

'Hello? Good morning? Anyone here?'

I could hear all right. I was just making a cup of tea when the brass bell rattled and announced an arrival.

'Hello Margaret? Charlotte. I'm a little earlier than I said I would be. Sorry.'

Charlotte is tall, skinny and wearing a printed headscarf around her scrawny neck. People always look different from how you imagine and she was no exception. I heard the crisp English on the phone but somehow imagined her short and plump, like a bruised apple. And here she was a fluttery thing with a beak like a crow. I squeezed between the Crimean war chest and tea boxes and stepped towards her.

'Books, you say? Well, I don't buy many. How many have you got?'

Charlotte plonked a wooden tomato box on a French polished table and I winced. I was about to move it but the box looked interesting and I ran my finger across the spines. 'I don't want the Readers' Digests. Not really. No one buys them. I know a man who will take them off you, he says people buy them by the yard.' I laughed. 'They buy them to fill their libraries. New money. Hah! Footballers' wives buy them to make themselves look clever. Have you ever heard anything so daft?'

Charlotte wasn't laughing. I cleared my throat.

'What's this? Let me see.' I pulled out a copy of Smoke Across the Fell by Graham Sutton and looked inside. Collins 1947. A little snort escaped. 'Tell you what, how about I give you £30 for the lot? I'm not being funny but these sell in Keswick market for about £3.'

'Oh!' Charlotte fluttered, she was obviously expecting more. 'Well perhaps...' She was clearly crestfallen and she asked, 'Could you possibly stretch to £40?'

'I'll meet you halfway. How about £35?' My son said I was a soft touch and I need to *get real* if I was ever going to make any money selling antiques, so I kept my face set and waited.

'Done!' Charlotte smiled.

I was going to offer a cup of tea but she wanted to leave as soon as I had counted out the money. I returned to the farmhouse leaving the books behind to look through another time.

******

It was a couple of days later when I got round to unpacking them. The box itself was almost an antique as it was lined with newspaper dating back to the 1950s. I pulled the faded broadsheet out, mindful of its age and read the adverts. How gullible folk were then! Adverts for almost anything you needed in a kitchen. Gadgets galore! Every woman should please her man. I almost missed the letter. Almost missed the prize. Tucked underneath the newspaper was an envelope, tied with blue ribbon and now faded from royal blue to duck-egg and it contained something. The date looked like 1930 but I couldn't be sure. I eased the brittle band off with care. Everyone likes to read a letter that isn't meant for them but I didn't open it straight away; I went and fetched a cup of tea and a fig roll and savoured the thought of what it might contain. I wasn't disappointed.

Oh, that tea's good. Reading glasses on. It says:

Dear Ruth,

As you have come to know, I am not one for flowery sentiment but the past few months have been a real pleasure. Our Friday meet-ups followed by fish and chip suppers have made me realise life is more enjoyable when it is shared. I don't have a lot to offer but I have a steady job that keeps me out of mischief. I am not a brave soul when it comes to talking to women. I have led a solitary life and find a letter is the easiest way for such a subject. I am afraid of making a fool of myself by asking you directly and so this is my cowardly approach. I wonder, dear Ruth, would you do me the honour of becoming my wife? I am acutely aware I have not done this correctly but wanted you to know of my intentions. I will propose properly in due course. I can offer the usual home comforts and pension when I'm gone.

Yours, AW.
PS My cat doesn't bite.

Well! I came over all giddy and had to sit down. That was a few months ago now. I contacted a dealer, an auctioneer chap via the internet (thank you Michael for educating me). My passport out of Hartside had arrived! I received a substantial cheque via a private buyer! Can you believe it? It allowed me to develop the upstairs of the barn into a very cosy home. I kept the business, of course, renamed it Wainwrights. Oh...and I put a loo in the back!

Sheep Dip

The only way to free her head from the continuing pattern of rows was to walk. Round and round the arguments would go, always arriving back at the same place. She had to walk the fells. It was the only place she ever wanted to walk, it was where she found her peace, her serenity and this was all part of the 'misunderstanding'. Misunderstanding was what her parents called it. There was no misunderstanding as far as she was concerned. Pakistan meant an arranged marriage and that was that. Not up for discussion they said. She queried the wisdom of a Western upbringing only to do an about-turn later in life and enslave her in custom.

Ashtani parked her car in the narrow lane, avoiding an entrance to a field; she thought her vehicle far enough off the road as a tractor had already squeezed through the gap earlier, yet the driver stared at her as she waited for him to drive by. Okay, so you don't get that many Asian women walking alone, but surely times were changing? She looked to the distant fells and gained comfort; they were like giant arms about her. She laughed, thinking she sounded like an advert for fabric conditioner and threw her rucksack on, the weight of it a simple pleasure like lugging a friend. Her job in advertising was never far away, she mused. She tilted her face up and tried to remember what warmth felt like. Air hurt as it raced up her nostrils, frozen like she'd gorged on kulfi. It was still early in the day, and early in the year. Shadows were deep and dark and her breath formed mini clouds as she huffed air out from her lungs. She carried on, creating more, pondering on how quickly they evaporated. The air smelled sharp, delicious. Of nothing. Just how she liked it.

The high fells beckoned, called her. It was ironic she had been named 'mountain lover'; she wondered if she had grown to fit it or whether it was meant to be?

Her family said, 'walking the fells was an obsession, something no respectable woman should do alone'. Her mother's heavily accented voice rang in her ear and she laughed an empty laugh and concentrated on placing her feet. The path was rocky, uneven and couldn't be seen for more than twenty yards, hidden by swirling mists that engulfed and muted all except for the crunch of stone. The forecast was good and Ashtani knew the clagg would lift, but right now it healed, kept her shrouded and safe. It would be very cold for a while longer as she was starting deep in shadow and was glad of her layers. The higher she walked, she knew she would shed layers of a different kind.

There was a dilemma ahead, a sodden, boggy patch spread for hundreds of yards and Ashtani wondered whether to take the long track skirting round or to retrace her steps and go across drier farm land. As far as she could tell from the map, the routes looked similar in length but the farm land had a footpath so it was an easy choice. Cloud was lifting so fast it was doubtful it had been there earlier. Sunlight flooded the high fells like someone had flicked a switch; the colour overwhelmed her, filled her with emotion she couldn't put a name to.

Something startled her. Something was splashing in the water. She couldn't see the beck as it was low down and between barbed-wire fences. She went to walk on but something was in there and she stopped and listened. Whatever it was, was big and splashing. She turned back.

'Oh hell!' Ashtani groaned, a well-rounded lamb ran neck deep in water. A fence cornered it, penned it with only yards before it was up against the wire. It panicked on seeing her, scrambled and clawed without footing on the bank, only to slip down, plunging into the water. It scratched at the mud slide once again and slithered, confused, back into the beck. The lamb was sodden and frightened. Ashtani knew it would exhaust itself and drown. Unless she helped.

'Great!' Wherever the farmhouse was, it was out of sight. She looked at her clothes and looked at the frantic animal as it struggled. Its head disappeared below water and quickly she undid her boots. It surfaced, sucked air and spluttered. It was getting weaker. 'Don't drown on me now, little one.' Ashtani glanced around; no one would see her slip off her trousers. She knew she could wear her waterproofs if need be; there wasn't time to switch right now.

She limbo'ed between taut new wire, catching her hair on a barb. The animal's bulging whites of eyes told of its terror, its panic in overdrive.

She had to be quick. If she reached without fuss, it would be better for the animal. She reminded herself, if she got the chance, to keep tight hold of its legs and to keep her centre of gravity low. When the animal made one last attempt to haul itself out of the ditch, she flung herself forward, made a grab and held fast. It struggled. It was stronger than she expected. Her face was pressed deep into the sopping greasy fleece and it felt rather wonderful. She held tight as it squirmed, not sure what her next move should be. It had to be quick, she was freezing. Getting a saturated lamb out of the ditch was not easy. It wriggled for its life. Not wanting to end up back in the water, she held on as tight as she could and tried to work out how best to get it over the barbed-wire which looked flesh-ripping taut. There was nothing for it but to lift it over by balancing on the lower stretch. The lamb struggled and she hoped her skin wouldn't puncture. Summoning a strength she didn't know she had (and grateful she still had her gym membership!) she gently lowered it and let it free. Her heart soared as it galloped off. There was no grateful turn to look at her, but that was okay.

She watched, marvelling at the spray that issued from the lamb's fleece as it ran, when a mud-spattered quad bike tore across the ground towards her, clods of earth flung up as it braked. Ashtani knew she looked ridiculous in her soggy socks, with her jacket barely covering her knees. She snatched at her boots as the man bellowed.

'What the bloody hell do you think you're doing? The path is over there!' he jabbed his finger towards the now sun-flushed fell. 'These fences cost money; they aren't for the likes of you to cross!'

She thought he added, 'Bloody walkers!' but couldn't be sure as he kept revving the bike. She hoped he hadn't noticed she was unshod and shivering; it was a distinct possibility with that temper getting in the way. Bare-legged and dithering, his rant was beginning to grate and she made herself count to ten in Cumbrian. It was a memorable skill; the trouble was she only recalled certain numbers like pimp, dick and bumfit. So apt, she almost smiled.

He yelled as he roared off, 'Offcomers' and 'proper paths', he gave no chance for her to explain.

'Tethera dick, lethera dick...' The simple act of counting, recalling ancient numbers and nuances from childhood helped. 'Hovera, Dovera, Dumbo...' Her vocabulary exhausted, she tugged on her waterproofs and shoved wet socks in the rucksack's side pocket. She debated returning to her car and perhaps abandoning the walk, but she was fed up of being shaped by others and after a bit of faffing about, managed to locate the original path where she began the long, steep ascent and breathed once more.

******

Looking through his binoculars, he spotted her. He tried to still his shaking hands as he spied the woman in the ripped, red jacket. She was along the top ridge. His hands betrayed him, betrayed too much. He knew the route well. It was simple enough and clear to see from the valley, unless she changed routes. He knew just how many kissing gates there were before reaching his father's land. It would be three hours before she would return and most of the time she would be in sight.

******

Ashtani tied her jacket around her waist and stuffed her fleece in her rucksack. It was now T-shirt weather, a rare and beautiful day with layered views that stretched forever. Alone felt good. She scrambled up a rock face, found a flat bit and hugging her knees tight, she felt safe. The valley stretched beneath her and she spotted a cluster of buildings where the angry farmer lurked and hoped she wouldn't run into him on her descent. She shook her head, freed her hair from her scarf and soaked up the bonus of April sun. A tiny, brilliant flash shone back at her, its dazzle hurting her eyes and she squinted as a miniature Land Rover bounced along a track. She watched the Lilliput world, satisfied it couldn't reach her. A crow circled above, eager for a crumb, its black wings ragged and it perched close by. She told it to wait until later and continued on to the summit.

Ashtani found the perfect lunch spot, a large swathe of short grass, now mown beautifully by Herdies where she sat and ate. Chapatti spilled out their contents of chopped onion and chutney and she picked up bits from the rock, chucked them into her mouth with an abandon she wasn't allowed at home. She licked her sticky fingers in defiance and munched on. Her map, a 'one in twenty-five' spread before her; she pored greedily over contours and crags, trigs and tarns, and plotted her descent. She adored maps. Always had. The family couldn't understand that either. She sighed, reluctant to move, reluctant to leave her blissful spot. Her family problems could wait; she put her feet up and shut her eyes. Five more minutes.

******

John Taylor busied himself. It was an empty busy-ness. He slung hay bales to his left and hay bales to his right, narrowly missing his dog. He cursed. He knew he'd been rude to the woman. He knew he should have at least listened. She must have been freezing. He smiled recalling her in her socks and wasn't devoid of sympathy. As he roared away, her words filtered through to him, but he was too irritated with himself and his family squabbles to turn back. Now feeling guilty, he decided he would meet the intriguing Asian woman. She was pretty cute.

******

When Ashtani spied the man in the grey boiler suit, she knew it was him and ducked behind a rock, kept her back to it. Her heart raced, she had to think of a way of getting past without him spotting her. She'd had enough of angry men. She peeped out and quickly tucked back in. He was still there. He was fetching things, hurrying backwards and forwards and every so often glanced in her direction.

'Damn!' She looked at her watch and considered another route, but knew she had pushed her luck not wearing socks. Blisters would not be far off.

'Damn!' She took a deep breath and stepped out. She had to. She tilted her head up; it was time to bluff it out before making her way down the rough path that snaked towards the farm.

******

John tried to be discreet. It wasn't easy. From the corner of his eye he could see her tip-toeing down. He fought the urge to stare, but didn't want to stall her and heaved himself up into his tractor cab, manoeuvring it so he could watch her in his wing mirror. He wiped slurry with his sleeve, picked off green bits and realised his nails were disgusting. Too late to run in now and wash them, he might miss her. He sat and tracked her delicate stepping, she would be down soon.

******

Ashtani felt her stomach knot and wondered why? She hadn't done anything wrong. In fact, she had done him a favour! But, she was glad he was turned away from her and hoped she could sneak round the side of the outbuildings without him noticing. Fixing her eyes on his back, she spotted a way and went for it! Her heart sank when he leapt out of the cab and ran towards her.

'Please...I'm sorry about earlier!'

His face looked different, altered. Pleasant perhaps?

'I realise I shouldn't have shouted at you and I wanted to say sorry.' He shrugged. He knew he shouldn't step nearer. There were undrawn lines. 'Can I offer you tea – by way of apology?' He pointed to a small, wrought iron table and three lichen covered chairs that had seen better days. One of them had a squished flat cushion. Her shoulders slumped in capitulation.

'There isn't any need to apologise...'

'I think there is. I was rude and aggressive. Please...' He gestured towards the table set with two chunky mugs, one of which had a chip too large to miss and she softened further. 'Have a cup of tea with me. It's the least I can do. You did rescue one of my sheep.'

His sheepish smile was better than his scowl Ashtani decided and swallowed hard. Stepping forward she accepted the English ritual in which she felt completely at home.

Storm Ahead

'You had better wash your hands.' Margaret was fussing as usual. I knew I ought to wash them more often, especially after handling the plants, but her nagging got on my nerves. It was all her bloody idea anyway.

I thought about our trip to Colorado last year; it was a good job our son could afford the fares, there was no way I could. He lived in a grand house, with far reaching views. I didn't like the area myself, too brown, everything's brown, not enough greenery. That's a laugh. He had enough greenery to...to...provide vitamin C to the Third World! It was like a bloody jungle. Margaret said it could change our lives for the better if we had a go. Too much to gamble I felt, but Margaret put her foot down.

I looked out of our window towards Clough Head, watched the rain sheet sideways and the fell hid its flanks behind grey cloud and I sighed; there was no comparison with those American mountains. They were big, too big and too dry.

Not for us. I'm glad Margaret prefers the Cumbrian ones. It's okay for her; she still has good legs and can get up them—albeit slowly.

She yelled from the side kitchen, 'I'm just going into Penrith! Make sure you check on things – that catch on the barn door needs sorting! Come on! Shift yourself! You can't sit around here all day when there's work to be done! And don't forget to wash your hands, especially when you go out. Dogs go berserk if they smell that on your fingers.'

I watched her lift the sagging cupboard door into place. I ought to try and fix that hinge again. A new kitchen is what she really wants. She walked towards me down the passage way, straightening the runner as she did. She had that look on her face that made me want to push her over, reminding me of a French Bulldog with her staring globular eyes. I loved her of course — she just irritated me no end. I waited for her to go out and start up the car before I moved. On principle.

Our cottage is remote, we were lucky to get it, prices being as they are in this part of the world, but Mum snuffing it just in time clinched the deal. Mell Views was ours. Poor old Mum, she was a good stick. Our smallholding allows us to grow our own veg; it's a bit different from the allotment, mind and a damned struggle at times, but I'm not too bad with brassicas now. I love a good kale. It was all trial and error. Five years down the road I didn't expect things to turn out as they have. Margaret and her bloody ideas.

'Trendy! Everyone's at it! Why shouldn't we do it as well? Make ourselves some real money!'

She had to be joking! But she wasn't and Mike sent us seeds. And that was it. Present from America. The plants look nice enough, mind and he helped us set things up via Skype. I'd never heard of hydro–bloody–ponics before! Margaret's never off the computer these days; no wonder her eyesight is bad. I still don't like the smiley face association though. I always believed drugs brought misery, but we have a mortgage to pay and the years are slipping by. Desperate times equal desperate measures. I looked at my watch; she would be at least an hour. I made a cup of tea, threw logs on the fire. I put the guard across, the wood I bought from our neighbour was too new, too green, it was spitting like a cornered cat. But, the warmth felt good. I like cosy. This room is dark and womb-like. Margaret doesn't like it for that reason, but those thick stone walls are solid and I feel quite safe from the howling wind.

******

'Did you fall asleep again?'

Oh heavens, I was in trouble.

'No Maggie, I was just having a little snooze.' I blew my nose to hide my face and tried to look like I'd been awake a while.

'You checked the barn door?'

'Of course I did! What do you take me for?' I tutted sufficiently for her to believe me and she disappeared to make a brew. I heard the gutter rattle and said I'd fix it when the wind had settled. Maybe tomorrow. I followed her into the kitchen and watched her put basics in the cupboard. She tied her apron strings and gave me a look.

'What's up now?'

'Look lively will you, there's two bags to unpack.'

'You know I always put things in the wrong places. You'll only move them again.'

Margaret smiled a tight-lipped smile that was more like a grimace; her eyes bulged once more.

'Well, you can pass me those things,' she said, 'save me bending down again.' Margaret straightened herself, rubbed the small of her back and laughed when I pulled out a triple pack of Baby Bio. 'It was on offer in that cheapy shop, I got six packs, only £4.99 for all those bottles. They looked at me a bit weird mind and I said you were into tomatoes.' Margaret laughed like a choking hyena when she got going and I left the room. There was another honk from the kitchen before she stomped through the passageway.

'Right, well that's that lot put away. Are you sure everything's okay over there, as it's a bit wild and I don't want to be going over again tonight?'

'Aye, everything's right as rain. Stop your worrying and sip your tea.' I pointed to the velour sofa opposite but she had other ideas and took her tea upstairs saying she would do a bit of sewing before the rest of the daylight disappeared.

I did wonder if everything would be okay. A power cut would bugger things up, but the barn was well insulated and it was chucking it down now. There was no real reason to worry. I'd have a look later.

The storm got worse and there was a lot of banging going on. Margaret and I chose to go to bed early, put the earplugs in and at least try and get a little bit of sleep. I dreamed of trees with evil smiling faces and branches reaching out to catch me — no explanation for that one! I slept in until 9am which wasn't like me. Margaret was still snoring; she always did if she was on her back. I lay still and listened. Things were still banging around but it was less vicious. At 9.40 I decided to move, I couldn't lie there any longer, I needed a pee. Of course I woke her up and was then blamed for letting her sleep in! You can't please some folk.

I took her a cuppa and placed it on the coaster – why we need coasters I don't know; the pine cupboard is so paint spattered it looks like an advert for Smarties. I retreated from her chatter, saying I was going to see if the Postie had been. He had. He'd left two brown envelopes, one white and a flyer for pizza. There was a card from the Post Office, saying they had knocked earlier but received no answer. A ticked box said a parcel had been left in the barn. The barn! That was an hour ago. Bloody Nora! I raced back upstairs and blurted out that the Postie had only been and opened the barn door! Margaret was barely awake but those eyes almost popped from their sockets. It was too late now. It was all too late. If only I'd locked the door. We were for the 'high-jump'. I could see the end of the drive from the window slowly, but surely, two police cars were wending their way up our lane.

The Fell Bragger

Was it totally inconceivable that I should be capable of bagging all of Wainwright's 214 fells? I knew I was capable; it appeared my family — that is my wife and children, didn't have as much faith. Come to think of it, neither did my friends. But that was thirteen years ago. That's how long it has taken to get to the point where I have a dozen or so summits to attain. I've tried to do a few each month, but as all Baggers know, the vagaries of the British weather will often alter plans and possibilities. And now I'm here in the Western fells. Looking up. They are biggies. I am not intimidated. I am not.

Back in The Dog and Gun — that quaint little pub in Keswick — the back slapping and bets pushed me into it. Too much beer and too little resistance. And the years slip by and people still ask, 'Have you finished them yet?' I ought to have said, 'Yes, I did them quietly, on my own. No celebration afterwards', and wave away any thought of congratulations, but I decided I'd have one last go, one last try to wrap this thing up.

******

The previous month was cold, snow lay in north facing pockets but I managed six, most of them in the Coledale round, some of them I'd done earlier. I'd even walked across the flanks of Grasmoor too – close-ish to the summit. I think that counts. As good as. A few yards off is okay isn't it? My next objective is Scoat, Red Pike and Yewbarrow. I'm camping here in Wasdale — close to the pub. The weather isn't too bad at all; the cloud line is well above the summits. There are quite a few other tents about, mostly those squat little green things used by the very keen. They don't have enough room for me. I prefer a bit of comfort and I like my food cooked — at the pub!

I think I have a lot in common with Alfred. He much preferred solo too. I understand his ethos; the beauty of the fells doesn't need chatter to set them off. My family know I'm here, know I'm going to finish tomorrow on Kirk Fell, but I insisted I finish alone. I think my friend Keith was quite put out but I convinced him it was something I wanted to achieve by myself.

'I'll join you!' he said, but as much as I like my friend, he gets on my nerves with all his gadgets and gizmos. I mean it's interesting, but he always thinks I want to know how many miles we've done, elevation attained, how long it took, etc. I wouldn't be surprised if his gadget told you your inside bloody leg measurement. I suppose I encouraged him really, back in the beginning when we started together. Maybe I should have asked him along, I feel a bit guilty, but he would insist I touch the cairn on each. As far as I'm concerned, you've bagged it if you come within 50 yards. Sometimes you just cannot get to the top if the conditions aren't right. That's suicidal. No, I know I've done the Wainwright's and that's what matters.

Putting my wife off was another thing altogether. Oh dear. Guilt is really setting in.

'Can't I come with you? This is silly,' her eyes were large and hopeful.

I understood where she was coming from. She had done quite a few with me. Her pathetic pleading almost made me change my mind, but these were the big ones. Huge chunks of rock. Stamina couldn't be plucked from the air and I wasn't sure she was up to it.

'No darling, it would be too strenuous. You know how tough the last few Western ones are going to be. Stay at home and think of me getting all wet and cold and I'll make it up to you when I get back.' I think I managed to placate her. Well, I thought I had.

'I've done most of them with you. I ought to be there at the end. I've never lagged behind. I don't understand.' I watched the shoulders slump.

I managed to convince her it was a very personal journey and I wanted to do the last few alone. We could go back together another time. I knew it didn't sound good and left shortly after breakfast. I made a quick getaway. Bless her, she'd packed my lunch. Wifey can join me on Sunday night when I'm back; I might take her for a basket meal. If I'm not too tired. She would like that.

******

This morning I folded my map into its concertina and stuffed it in my plastic wallet, strung it around my neck and set off for Overbeck Bridge; it was quite a walk.

Scoat Fell is a funny one. The cloud was down so I couldn't quite see the cairn. I know it's set into the wall. It's an unusual position. I've seen it in all the books so I know what it looks like. I touched the wall lower down near a pile of stones but decided not to clamber up any further. What's the point? You can't see! If Keith had been with me he would have said, 'Not far now, not far, just another little scramble.' And we would have touched the cairn and not had any views anyway.

That's another ticked off.

Yewbarrow was interesting though; there are two cairns up there. I did them both as they were more or less en route. I feel quite proud of myself today. It was wet underfoot but my boots still have a bit of life in them, they should see me through tomorrow. I probably won't buy another pair. Good night. Hope the bed bugs don't bite.

******

Well, today is the day! My last couple of AW's lie ahead. Ah, what a grand day it is. It's clear enough, perhaps there's a bit of light cloud. I would ring wifey if there was a signal. I'm going to go up Gable, my penultimate, along Moses Trod, turn up close to Gable Beck and I'll traverse down to Beckhead Tarn where I might eat my lunch then stop a while on Kirk Fell. Kirk Fell is a fine mountain to finish on. It looks like a proper mountain, wide at the bottom and tapers nicely, like a cone all the way to the shelter at the summit. A chunk of Toblerone. Back in a bit and I'll tell you how it went.

******

Crickey Bloody Moses Trod! The Wasdale Head is full of people!

'Surprise! Well done! Fantastic! We couldn't stay away! 214! 214! Yaaayyy!

What an achievement!'

'What?' People everywhere. 'What?' Folks are slapping me on my back. It registers. I can see my wife, clapping, smiling. My son too, at the back, craning his neck, grinning. Everyone is looking at me, even the barman is grinning. The bloody bastards. I've been set up. Hell's teeth, there's Keith.

'Hi Tom, yeah, yeah, it was fantastic thanks. Yeah, yeah, it was clear, great views. Thanks, yeah, yeah. Oh, hi Sue, what are you doing here? Sorry daft question. You buggers! You rotten bloody lot. Oh God, not candles on a cake too.'

Keith isn't smiling, well, he has that half-smile he sometimes does. He's looking a bit po-faced, a bit pissed off in fact, probably because I didn't want him with me. Or maybe he's a bit envious as he has another forty or so to do.

'Hey Bob, nice of you to come. What? Yeah, hi Jim.'

Well, I never expected this. Wifey is well proud. Perhaps I'm forgiven.

'Speech! Speech!'

Oh gawd.

'Thanks everyone. I don't deserve this, especially as I shooed you all away. Completing the Wainwright fells for me has been a marvellous journey; every step of the way has been a joy. You know it has taken me years to finish, but I'm glad it's done and I can get back to doing my favourites with my favourite person, my lovely wife. Thank you.'

I ducked out, gave Sheila a squeeze and went to the gents'.

'Over here!' Keith wanted something. 'Over here.' He waggled his fingers at me and I walked over. Someone shoved a pint in my hand.

'Who the hell organised all this?' I asked, thinking Keith may be behind it.

'It was Sheila's idea,' Keith wouldn't look me in the eye.

'How did you know what time I'd be back at the pub?'

He looked at me square-on like it was painful for him and said, 'I know you laugh at me for my gadgets. Well, I bought these just recently.' Keith fished out a couple of two-way radios from the top of his rucksack.

'Oh! That was clever of you.' I felt a bit sick.

'Did you see anyone up there?' Keith nodded in the general direction of where I'd come from and was now scrutinising my face. He must have known I skirted Gable.

'I didn't see a soul. Not a soul.'

'Didn't you see a guy with a bright orange jacket?'

'Now you come to mention it, there was someone with an orange jacket. Do you know him? Is he in here?'

'That was me. I knew it would work. I bought a new one, knew you wouldn't recognise me in it if I kept a safe distance and with a black hat on it worked. I was able to let them, let Sheila and everyone else down here know just where you were.'

I panicked. 'You let them know?'

'Yes. More or less.' He nodded, 'Can you just move a bit to your left?'

'What? Why?'

'I want to take your picture. More to the left. Yeah, stand just there.' He clicked away. 'That's it recorded for posterity.'

'What is?'

'You are. There's a poster behind you.' Keith shuffled, his lips pursed, chin jutting upwards. 'Have you seen it before?'

I shuffled, keeping my eye on him, not knowing where he was coming from.

'It's all about a guy who used to come here. He won a competition many, many years ago. He's quite famous. Will Ritson. Does the name ring a bell?'

'No, no, not at all.' I turned around. Scanned the words.

The Grand Seal of the Order of Wasdale
having proved to be
Public Contest
Will Ritson
The Biggest Liar in The World

The Locksmith's Daughter

She stood, half hidden by the tree, ate her 'Delicious Ambleside Ice Cream' and watched as a group of Spanish tourists passed her by. They were swiftly followed by Japanese who trailed obediently in their camera-clicking wake. She spotted a few potentials and as she perused the people before her, she plunged her tongue into the cold scoop, its chill always a treat. She lingered, as folk headed to the pier. There were enough single, older men who would do the trick and she took the Hunter from her pocket and checked the time. Five more minutes. It was the most accurate watch ever, never lost a second! Reliable like nothing else! She held the chain up and the fob twirled, catching the light as it whirled one way then the other. Her eyes glinted, reflecting her pleasure as it sparkled and she tucked it deep in her pocket.

It was warm, the tourists were out in their droves and with her walking boots on and ice cream in hand, she could be anyone. Disregarded, faceless, invisible. Just how she liked it. Little Miss Overlooked.

Anna bit the end of her cone and sucked hard allowing the cream to ooze down her throat. She and Daddy used to race each other, see who would finish first. She invariably lost. It was stupid really; it always made her head hurt. Freezer burn or something? But that was a long ago memory and now she could wait for the ice cream to soften and slip down. She nodded, scoring a point and knew her dad would be smiling too.

It was time to run, the boat was about to depart. Her timing had to be perfect and she ran as fast as she could. Speed plus drama always worked and with her arms flailing and wild pointing towards the soon to depart vessel, she shouted, 'John, you've got my ticket!' The jetty was slippery but she assessed correctly that there were too many pensioners about for it to be unsafe and she lunged towards the small, now cordoned off section. 'John, my ticket!'

Invariably the ruse worked, the perplexed man would let her through and she would step across the gangplank before it was pulled. She tripped nimbly down steps into the saloon and picked out a man to sit by, someone nondescript who had his back to the majority and she snuggled as close as she dared without making him uncomfortable enough to move. Sometimes they would talk and she would speak softly but usually pulled down her hat or tugged a strand of hair across her face and kept herself to herself.

******

Wray Castle was an impressive shell of a place; there was nothing much to take but she knew that was when people dropped their guard, thinking there was little of value. There was always something for the picking.

From the boat, she followed the herd, kept close with the tight little group, kept pace up the front steps to the ticket desk and apologised for her husband having gone on ahead with hers. 'Oh, he does this all the time. I'll just get mine from him and come back. I'm so sorry, I won't be a minute.' She was too respectable to be questioned and sailed through.

People were milling in the airy hall, staring up at the vaulted ceiling waiting for the next tour to begin. She stole into the shop and was gratified to see no cameras, no mirrors, no nothing. There was only one person looking after things and right now she was bent down restocking a shelf. Anna did not acknowledge her, kept her face turned away, yet in her peripheral vision she knew she had been spotted, weighed up as decent and ignored. Women of a certain age and bearing could get away with anything, she chuckled.

Time was of the essence and before her, on the counter, sat a tray of pretty brooches. Someone had carelessly left them unattended. How silly. How trusting.

One, two, three, in they go. Face away from assistant. Time to exit. Out the door. Woman on the desk has left her post. How trusting are the National Rust! Anna ran and caught the next boat.

******

Back in Ambleside, she steeled herself to walk past the cake shop without buying, held her breath so as not to get a whiff and could breathe once more by the time she reached the very quaint and dinky Bridge House. She headed towards the steeply twisting road aptly named: The Struggle. She chuckled, knowing she looked like any other walker with her boots, waterproof jacket, rucksack and poles. Head down. It was the perfect cover. No one noticed. She smiled as the cottage came into view. It wasn't overlooked by any other building. Her homework on the internet had paid off once more. Today was Saturday, and yesterday, just before Cumbrian Cottage Breaks had closed, she rang and enquired about a last minute deal for the weekend. 'Sorry, no, that cottage is taken, we have a few others in Ambleside we can give you a discount on...'

And her answer was always the same, 'Shame I really fancied Ghyll Cottage, I'll call again, maybe next week.' That was after they had told her the cottage she really wanted – along with others – was vacant. Simples.

The narrow path down the right hand side of the cottage ate deep into the fell-side; the rear was dark, and if truth be told: slimy. But its cover was perfect; the back room had French windows barely letting in enough natural light so no one would notice her candle. It was always a candle; it could be blown out if she detected foot-steps. It didn't take long to work the lock. It never did. She was in.

Today's pickings weren't bad; the gift shop on her way back through town was easy to plunder. Anna examined her hoard and knew just how much she would get on eBay. Yes, it had been a good day. She walked into the little box room at the back of the house and pulled off her wig. She threw it on the over-painted Lloyd loom chair and removed the pillow from the narrow bed, carefully placing it on the floor. As always, she lay on top without disturbing the cover as much as possible. It was a practiced art and it would only need straightening the next day. The single room at the rear, with its quaint wooden features, was perfect for her needs. The idea was to stay for free, pocket a few choice items and leave without anyone noticing she had ever been there. Her rucksack was large and accommodating. It always contained her own squished duck down pillow. It would be too much of a clue to leave behind an imprint of her head or stray hairs. She settled back and by the glow of her candle, twirled the fob watch round and round above her head and as she had done many times before, read the engraved message on the back:

To Dad, Happy 65th.

The best Locksmith in the World,

and kissed it.

The next day, before she left, she nicked a loo roll from the bathroom, pinched the batteries from the mantel clock and pocketed a small china vase. It wasn't Moorcroft but might fool some. Oh yes, and that little flat-back ornament on the shelf – that would fetch a bit. It was the sort of thing the cleaners would overlook – well – for a little while, she chuckled.

******

Kendal's aptly named festival – Mintfest (the home of the famous oversweet cake) was gearing up and the streets were filling with people in party-mode. Easy pickings. She could make a mint. Anna laughed at her little joke and assessed the crowd. It was building nicely. She would go and get a coffee before making a start.

A jewellers-come-gift-shop caught her attention and she lifted a necklace for the hell of it, but it had been a close call and as soon as she could, she reversed her coat and changed her wig for the red one. It clashed with her jacket, but it was a small price to pay. Anna slipped deep into the crowd. It was all elbows and acrid armpits. Dizzy and intoxicated, she was swept along and clapped in time to the pounding music of a magic act. Blank faces stared back, Venetian masks betrayed nothing. Time was moving on but this was amazing. A juggler in a harlequin outfit whirled flaming batons. Trapeze artists swooshed on temporary apparatus and fireworks banged and fizzed. Smoke hid truth and trickery. A monkey screeched and she dug her hands deep in her pockets.

It wasn't there.

It wasn't in the right one where it usually was. It wasn't in the left. She checked the right again and threw her jacket off, checking all pockets that were normally on the outside. It had to be there. It had to be. But the fob had gone. It was no longer in her pocket. She screamed and shook her fist at the sky but no one heard; she was just another fun-seeker, yet some lousy, stinking, thieving scumbag had taken the only thing that mattered and she kicked her rucksack hard, kicked it harder and raged at the sky. Raged at the injustice of it all. Spittle slipped down her chin as she shook her fist at everyone and no one. Everyone laughed and clapped. But she was invisible. She kicked her rucksack until her feet hurt. Pilfered china cracked and split.

'Bastards! Cheating lousy bastards!' She whirled round, lashing out at the hand that gripped her shoulder and thrashed against the restraining force. Her wig slipped sideways and she couldn't see. Nothing made sense until a radio crackled some mumbo jumbo and she slumped gratefully, at last someone would now be able to help her. Through snivelling snotty sobs she said, 'Help me. I've been robbed!'

The Lollipop Lady

Jennifer really was a reasonable woman. But that all changed when planning permission was granted for forty-six houses the other side of her fence.

Jennifer's small-holding belonged to her parents before her; it had been in the family for over 80 years and was a blissful, unspoilt patch of perfection. Through the gate in her fence she would walk, follow the sheep trod down to the pond and watch wildlife through scratched binoculars. The Eastern fells were still just in view. Fields rolled until they reached rock, but the view was only in one direction now. The narrow passage of green was shrinking and Jen felt increasingly desperate.

There was often a mixture of wildlife to be seen, wildlife that crossed territory in its search for food, its natural terrain was decreasing with man's encroachment. Her own situation was no different. She sighed and looked at her watch. It was 6.15am and light; the builders would be starting soon and she needed to get back and wipe down her uniform, ready to start the day. There were only a few days left before the children broke up for school and she would have six weeks in which her time would be her own.

She drove for five minutes and turned sharply into the school car park. It was early and she sat for ten before pulling 'the lollipop' from the rear of her Kangoo. She poured tea from her flask and watched as windows opened and closed in the small primary school, knowing the cleaners hadn't left yet. She knew the school wouldn't last, it was Victorian and someone somewhere would want progress and tear the thing down. Many years ago she too had attended the school and felt part of its fabric. Jennifer looked at her watch again. Five more minutes. She sipped tea, looked up at the roof and was soothed by the slope of the large purple/black tiles. She loved their scalloped edges and chuckled at her old childish thoughts: they were the ridge on a dinosaur's back. The solid sandstone was wearing away with reckless speed but it was familiar and safe. Someone rapped on the window and she slopped her tea.

'Hi Jen. You looked miles away there!' Paula was on her way out and always said hello.

'I was. I was just thinking about my time here.' She laughed as she mopped her leg with a tissue, 'Long ago now!'

'Aye. Happy days, hey? See you.'

Paula waddled off. Jennifer sat another two minutes and gnawed on a garibaldi.

After her morning shift safely crossing children outside All Saints Parish, she drove home thinking about progress and all the word implied. She believed it a march no one could halt. Her own situation was too far down the road to alter now but resentment burned deep, festered away without a soul knowing the true depth of her feelings. It wasn't fair.

She pulled into her drive and was grateful for the main part, it still wasn't overlooked, yet everything was caked in builder's dust and she trailed a finger across the roof of her late father's car. She slammed her front door harder than she meant.

******

At 7pm she wandered over the site. It was easy. All she had to do was pull aside her larch panel and she was in. The circumference screamed, NO ENTRY, TRESPASSERS WILL BE PROSECUTED, but she smiled wryly thinking no one could insist on a hard hat for her. She picked her way across the temporary rubble-impacted access road and headed towards half-built houses. Plastic flapped in the breeze but that was the only movement on the strangely silent site.

Jennifer walked into what she imagined to be a potentially pretty little lounge and wondered who would live there. It was small and dark and had a view of next door. She shuddered and went out. A crow watched her and when it cawed, she shouted back to it, 'Aye. I know. It's an absolute disgrace!' When she found a pack of half-eaten sandwiches, she took them out and threw them towards her familiar. It flew off. 'Suit yourself,' she shrugged and dusted her hands.

Someone had left a hammer behind; she turned it over, examined it before stuffing it in her pocket and wandered over to a half-built window. She checked over her shoulder before putting her foot to the new wall. She pushed hard until bricks tumbled outwards onto a heap of builder's sand. 'What a shame,' she said.

She swung through scaffolding, dipped between planks and ladders and looked towards ponies in the field and muttered, 'Horses through courses.' Her humour just intact and with sadness, looked back at her own piece of land and realised the next layer of bricks would allow the inhabitants a view of her home. A clear view. Panic welled once more. She couldn't bear the idea of being overlooked and worried a scab on her arm, scratched it until it bled. The Developer had made a paltry offer for her four acres; perhaps she should have accepted, but she knew nowhere else, this was her home and she would die here. There was nowhere else to go.

The larch panel was pulled back into place and secured with a brick. Jennifer checked her chickens and trailed down towards 'the hole'. Once upon a time it ate a fridge. It took a month. Nothing was ever regurgitated. Nothing burped back. She threw the hammer in, watched it bounce and settle. It wasn't always obvious the earth was moving, but if she came back in an hour it would be gone. Sucked down goodness knows where. The process had speeded up since the builders had shifted earth around. Jennifer hoped it wouldn't get any bigger. She watched fascinated by the slow slipping of soil, the gentle movement of earth creeping towards the centre where it turned in on itself. The hammer looked like it was crawling, like it had tiny centipede legs. The heavy end slipped under quickly and the handle shot upwards in protest. She watched it sink like an arm, clinging defiantly to its last moment of life. This time it took all of three minutes. Horrified, she ran to her back porch and pulled the bolt across, stood with her back to the door, realising with some irony, her heart was indeed hammering. She poured a large finger of Teacher's. The mirror above the fireplace reflected a paler than usual face. Nothing new. Her unruly hair was its usual mess, always trying to escape her wide-brimmed hat. She pulled it off, twisted an orange lock around her little finger and clipped it into submission. It promptly fell out, she growled, said a naughty word her dad wouldn't have approved of and poured another whisky.

******

The following morning, builders started work an hour earlier than usual and she was only just back through the fence before the noise started. Bang! Bang! Bang! She clapped her hands over her ears, shrieked loud and long and then a practised mantra of pseudo Buddist chanting gushed forth from her before she got ready for work.

'Good morning, Jennifer!'

'Morning, mums and children!'

It was a familiar routine. Jennifer stood holding her lollipop, checked both ways for stragglers before thanking motorists. In another five minutes she could go home. She had been doing the same job for the last twelve years. At least she was outdoors. That was the best bit about the job, but she was fed up of it now. The worst was the car fumes. There would be so much more traffic when the estate was completed. A car tooted and she waved thinking it was someone she knew but a youth drove by giving her the finger. *Get stuffed* she mouthed in her head. What was wrong with kids today? Retirement felt like a good option.

When she returned home, Jennifer closed all her windows. Radio One was too much. The men's shouting drowned out their radio and their radio was turned up. She reported the earlier start to the council.

She decided she would work in her front garden, perhaps get some respite, hoping it might be a little quieter there, but the intermittent, strangulated yelling that the builders thought of as 'singing' carried a long way. Working in the front made no difference to the sound levels and Jennifer sloped indoors and sat with hands clamped over ears, staring at her shag-pile. She sat without moving for what seemed like a very long time before ringing the council once again. They said they would come out, but couldn't stipulate when.

******

A few days later, after her stint at school, a man stood in her drive holding an official-looking clipboard. He wore a suit and a hard hat, yet didn't look like he was from the council. His suit was too sharp.

'Mrs Weston?'

'I am when I'm at home.'

'I'm from Affordable Habitats.' The man proffered a hand which she looked at but decided not to shake. He coughed and fidgeted in his pocket for a card. He held it towards her and Jennifer accepted it like she would catch something from merely holding it. She turned it over and read every word. Twice. She squinted up at him; he was tall and standing in front of the sun and when he spoke he asked if they could chat somewhere else. She replied: where they were was fine.

His mouth looked smarmy; she watched saliva gather in the corners, 'Blah, blah, blah, apologies, blah, blah, blah, will speak to the men, blah, blah, blah, hope to be best of neighbours, sorry, blah, bloody, blah.' And off he went. She slammed her door and the letterbox rattled like it agreed with him. Like it was on his side.

'Shut up!' she yelled at her door.

******

She was glad she had put in a letter of resignation. It was the right thing to do. Change was needed. She glanced around her '70s bungalow. It was worn, tired and in need of TLC, not unlike herself. The builders hadn't started yet. It was quiet for the moment and today's noise would only go on until 2pm – being a Saturday – that's when they were due to finish. She could hold out until then. Perhaps she would tidy the place up, get the hoovering done over their noise? Put her own radio on? Perhaps enjoy her weekend? There would be some peace later and tomorrow – Sunday, would at least be builder-free.

******

By 3pm she was crying. By 4pm she felt murderous. At 5pm she ran down the garden and screamed at the nearest builder.

'What?' A man cupped his ear and turned the radio down to hear her better.

'Can you PLEASE turn that noise down? Preferably off!' She realised he already had.

'Oh, sorry love.'

The builder turned, looked like he said something to the man next to him and they laughed. She imagined it was a derogatory comment and pounced, 'You aren't supposed to be here now! You aren't supposed to be working this afternoon!'

The man shrugged and began cutting up long lengths of wood. His mate zapped his air-gun into laths.

'Where's your boss?' Jennifer demanded between blasts of pneumatic air. She could hardly hear herself speak.

The men looked at her and pointed towards the cabin. Jennifer went back through her home, leaving her front door wide open and raced around to the metal pens that surrounded Affordable Habitats. Bright coloured flags flicked and flapped with happy family faces. They were mocking her. Perfect giant teeth grinned down.

'Hello? Hello? Can you let me in?' She rattled their cage. 'Hello?'

There was no one to be seen. She could hear them and saw there were half a dozen cars tucked together on the dusty drive and a light was on in the port-a-cabin. She wanted to throw a brick, instead a furious, strangulated scream issued from her throat. In fury, she ran back home.

A sleepless night ensued. At 3.30 am she got up and looked out of her bedroom window, the distant fells were bathed in moonlight. It was perhaps best when she couldn't see anything. In the dark, she felt for her slippers and went and made warm milk before crawling back into bed. Sleep wasn't going to happen and she flicked on her bedside lamp and counted the plaster swirls on the ceiling. Forty-two. She knew there were 42. Her dad's handiwork.

By 9am she felt drained. By 9.15 it started.

Jennifer ran to the calendar in the kitchen. She knew it was a Sunday yet Led Zepplin was belting out the words, 'And she's buying a stairway to heaven...'

'I'll give them a bloody stairway to hell in a minute! I've had no sleep. No rest. No peace.' She kept up the chant as she ran with her hitched up nightie scrunched in her hands.

Jennifer didn't try going in the front entrance, she ran straight to the bottom of the garden, pushed aside the larch-lap and squeezed into enemy territory. She picked up half a brick. Looking left and right she couldn't see a soul and followed the sound as it grew louder. And there he was, crouched over something, a solo builder, oblivious to her sneaking. It was when he yelled out the chorus that she struck. She smashed his skull again and again and again until she was sated and stood until her breathing settled. She had no emotion left. Blood oozed. She stood blinking in the sharp morning light, watched his drips fall before the brick slipped from her fingers. Her filthy night-dress flickered on a stray breeze, its embroidered flowers poppy red. Convinced he was working alone; she turned to run, stopped herself and rubbed her eyes, and blinked rapidly. It was real. He was lying there. He was so still, he was probably dead. Thoughts of the hole wouldn't leave her mind. She couldn't. Could she? The hole was perhaps the only solution? The only one. He was probably less than ten stone. She could do it, couldn't she?

The radio cut in:

I hope you are all having a wonderful Sunday whatever you are doing! It's a great day for a BBQ all you lucky people out there enjoying the sun. We have a fantastic selection of music for you this morning to help ease you into your Sunday. If the Led Zep didn't wake you sufficiently – how about a little of this...

Jennifer did not think the DJ's next choice was funny, U2's Sunday, bloody Sunday sprang her into action and she flung the dead man's arm around her shoulder and tugged. He didn't budge. She grabbed him by his boots, tried dragging – but that didn't work either. She ran towards the doorway looking for inspiration.

And then she saw it.

She'd spotted a wheelbarrow and raced it back over the uneven ground as quickly as she could, getting as close to the doorway as possible. The limp man wasn't making it easy. 'Get your builder's bum in there, will you!' She folded in the crumpled lump as best she could and remembering the brick, dropped it on his crotch. He wasn't going anywhere! The radio still blared and in one last fit of anger she battered it until it screamed no more.

With orange hair streaming behind, she rushed with as much strength as she could muster. In her voluminous, blood-encrusted night-dress Jennifer ran, yet viewed herself from afar like an extra in a movie. Except she really was hurrying along with a large black wheelbarrow, its bright yellow wheel squeaking with every revolution. And there was a man in it. A very lifeless man.

It must have taken ten minutes from the time she bashed in his head to the time she got to her fence. Knowing it wasn't big enough to get the barrow through, she rammed it as hard as she could. Nothing gave way, except the man's head lolled with every lunge. The brick rolled off. She wheeled backwards half a dozen steps and took a raging run. The man flopped sideways and fell onto the baked earth. Jennifer, further enraged, kicked and kicked at the panelling until pieces cracked, splintered and finally gave way. She pulled and tugged at fencing until there was just enough of a man-sized space to haul Jo Bloggs through. He was getting heavier and she hitched up her skirts to wipe her brow.

The hole was ten yards away, gaping and hungry. Soil trickled as it slipped towards the unsated stomach. She sat, caught her breath and remembering the brick, she walked calmly back to the broken fence and retrieved it. She flopped close to the bloodied man and wondered how best to lift him the last few feet. She was running out of energy and ideas. She winced at the ubiquitous checked shirt, (why did they have to wear them?) and from the front gripped it with both hands and pulled. The body sat upwards, bent at the waist and she lowered him back down flat whilst she thought through the next bit. With her hands still in place she felt warmth from his chest and for the first time realised how young he was. About 22. His scrappy beard barely covered his chin; she swallowed and hunkered closer, tried to get her arms underneath. It was all too late. With every ounce of strength she possessed she lugged him closer to the edge. Her face was close to his and unexpectedly, he smelled fresh: of toothpaste. She winced at his blood-encrusted hair. When his breath brushed her cheek, she dropped him. He was still alive.

Jennifer looked at her brown stained hands and willed them to stop shaking. It was impossible. Her eyes sprang wide when his phone trilled a silly tune and danced its way out of his pocket. A picture of a smiling baby flashed insistently. Daddy.

Daddy. Daddy. She waited for the Happy Nipper to stop calling before picking it up and dialled 999.

Calmly she asked for an ambulance, thanked them very much and switched it off. She tucked it back in his pocket, fastened the button and patted it in place. She cradled his head and whispered, 'I'm sorry.' And with breathless speed she took a running leap into the centre of the hole. She knew it would all be over before the police arrived.

Wannabe Sam

Since his divorce, Sam tramped the fells with his dog more often. He knew Bonny was good enough for SARDA. She was a damned fine dog, strong and fit with an excellent nose and could find anything or anyone – but he wouldn't humiliate himself with putting her forward again! He'd keep her for himself. Just the two of them. They didn't need anyone else.

'Go on Bonny!' He lobbed a ball as far as he could; it hit a rock and changed direction. Bonny barked and careered after it. She dropped it at his feet. He didn't know where he'd be without his wee friend. He patted her and threw it again. She wasn't so little really. She was a golden retriever and could do with losing a few pounds. But she was fit and healthy. It didn't matter; she needed the extra fat in the blue chill.

His chosen path up from Middle Dodd was worn and slippery, in parts deeply eroded and water trickled under creaking ice. Sam continued upwards, aware of splintered crunching, shards shattering and cracking beneath his boots. He looked across at Caudale and beyond, the higher fells were still snow-capped. Twenty yards ahead, Bonny turned and watched him, she stared, panting and steaming waiting for him to catch up and when satisfied he was following, ran off.

When Sam reached Red Screes summit he took off his rucksack and called her. He tugged at his gloves with his teeth, thumped his hands together, blew on them before he unfolded his sit mat; a little comfort wasn't a bad idea. It was time for a hot drink. He couldn't see Bonny but knew she wouldn't be far away. As he unwrapped foil from fruit cake, she nuzzled his arm and he broke a piece off. Predictable, lovely Bonny was on-cue. She would do anything for food. He threw the ball for her and unscrewed his flask. Looking West, the Scawfel range from the trig point was a feast for sore eyes and he drank in the view along with his coffee and stared unblinking at the white and blue and still and cold, the lonely and the saddest of vistas. He thumped his hands once more and hoped mountain rescue wouldn't take too long in reaching their decision: they needed a man like him with his experience and know-how. He knew he was fit, knew his map and compass skills were up to date; he was good with a GPS. What wasn't to like? He didn't want more rejection but still hoped he could become a member of the local mountain rescue team and awaited their decision. They were taking their time

Bonny arrived at his feet, her eyes large and round and she nosed the slobber-covered ball in his direction. It was the only thing that wasn't frozen. Sam laughed, ruffled her fur and took a dog biscuit from his pocket, the ball forgotten as she gobbled the morsel. He pulled her to him, checked the Velcro straps on her jacket were secure and pushed her away.

'Right! Where shall we go after this young lady? Shall we go down towards the pub or shall we go up there?' Sam nodded towards Dove Crag. Bonny looked at him and trotted in the direction of the Inn. He smiled and shrugged, the decision made. He would head east and follow the mutt. The gully known as Kilnshaw Chimney it was.

There was a lot of snow. It was sparse in the valley, but the fell tops were crisp and sparkling. There was a fair six inches underfoot. It was freezing and still. The horizon was yellow, cold egg-yolk yellow with black smudges spreading. He pulled his hat over his ears and vowed to buy a better one, a thicker one; this one had shrunk and it kept riding up. That, or his head had grown. His icy blue world was silent. And black. And still. He knew when more colour returned to The Lakes, along with the spring, people would return, return to his private world. Winter was his favourite season as he didn't have to share his beautiful kingdom. He didn't dislike people, but preferred winter walkers best. Most nodded, kept their heads down and didn't need to pass the time of day. Not like in the summer when everyone wanted to know where you had come from and where you were going. It was like Blind Date. He had no time for idle chat.

From the cairn, Sam took a photo. A selfie for Facebook and added drama by rubbing snow into his moustache. He grinned, 'one to show the guys'. Bonny was out of sight but he saw her tracks and followed. He knew he was good at that. Her paws had sunk deeply, at least four inches. She was easy to follow. He chuckled; she was carrying enough weight to make an impression even though the snow was hard. A lighter dog might have skipped over the surface without a trace. Sam sensed where she might be heading, she could probably smell food. It was time to go into the valley. He assumed the pub would be open and he could maybe have a quick drink, a wee snifter, before deciding where to head next. He followed the prints and fascinated by the purity of their form, he slipped and rolled before picking himself up and dusting himself down. The dog couldn't be seen, but the trail headed towards the edge. Under normal conditions the path was straightforward, steep but not difficult. It needed more care this time of year. It was lethal today. He shouted for Bonny and thought he should change his route, perhaps go back the way he came but he couldn't see her. He yelled but everywhere was still and silent. The air heavy and contained like he couldn't puncture it. His voice wouldn't travel. He called again, 'Bonny! Bonny!' There was nothing but crushing silence. He ignored his stomach knotting. Where was she?

It was 4pm and light was fading; he reckoned he had another hour max before it was dark. He looked at his watch. He would be fine. He cursed the dog for running off. Dark cloud was heading his way. Fast. The tiny pub was hundreds of feet below and he looked hard to detect a glimmer. The car park had quite a few vehicles and he wondered how many were die-hards like himself. It started to sleet. They couldn't be tourists, surely most were like himself – people who knew how to handle winter. He snorted and eyed the path. Another few yards, yes, the dog had gone the difficult way, down the gully. It would be three points of contact all the way. He knew his stuff. Sam consoled himself with the tricky descent. He would enjoy it. He was rapidly running out of light and probably wouldn't get beyond the pub so this would have to satisfy him for the day. Paw prints had disappeared but he knew the way and began the slow descent. It was icier than anticipated.

'Bloody dog. What have you got me into this time?' He spat the words out as his fingers groped for hand-holds, grasped at rimed rock. It was very slow going. A piece fractured, came away in his hand and he shook his head and smiled knowing it was easy to be caught out by crumbly rock. He examined it closely for a moment and let it drop, watched it bounce and shatter before it came to a standstill in soft snow. Hand over hand he descended, wishing he'd brought his ice axe and crampons.

'Oh well. They weren't needed earlier,' he muttered, ignoring the fact his heart was hammering and blood throbbed in his ears. He shrugged and looked over his shoulder down the gully. He couldn't see the pub; three sides of rock entombed him. He assured himself he was okay...until he lost his footing and slipped and slithered, bounced and hit something hard. He bounced again, rolled and twisted. Slid and tumbled. And stopped. Thank goodness he was caught. He'd live. He felt his face. It was all right but he'd bumped the back of his head and his hat was gone. Snow packed his nostrils and he blew hard and spat out red snotty blood. It spattered the rock close by. He thought it made an interesting pattern and felt his head, unsure if he was bleeding or not; he couldn't tell with his black gloves on and he couldn't reach anything he could smear.

He took a deep breath and tried to assess how far he'd fallen. He'd landed upright with his back to the gully and estimated he'd travelled a good twenty feet and was now hanging, swinging slightly and counted himself lucky. He tried to move but was held fast. His right foot hung limply and he shuffled it to the left, felt with his toes for something solid. He slid his left foot further left and managed to slide his right a little towards it, but couldn't get a grip on the ice. He barely had a toe-hold and tried to turn. It was impossible and he didn't understand why. It didn't add up. He wriggled vigorously, conscious he could drop at any moment and panic rose. He swallowed hard.

'What?' He thrashed again, tried to wrench himself free but it wasn't working. He was stuck.

'Shit.' He was in deep do-do and told himself to breathe. Keep calm. Snared by his rucksack, he dangled. He chided himself, knew he should have kept facing the rock as he came down, shouldn't have turned to look at the pub which could no longer be seen. Blasted bloody dog! 'Bonny! Bonny!'

He wriggled again and his right foot slipped further and he lost the little footing he had altogether and swung gently, creaking as the strap tightened. It hurt. Images of parachutists caught in trees floated through his mind. Could he unclip his hip belt and slip his shoulders out, would he fall and bounce much further? That was not going to happen. The drop was too great. Kilnshaw Chimney would claim him.

'Bonny! Here girl! Bonny! Bonny! Sodding hell! Bonny! Bonny!' His shivering was out of control and he thought of the whistle in his pack. If only he could reach it. He knew he had a torch...

A tear trickled down his face and he whimpered and told himself to get a grip. Think it through! Come on man, you will be okay. What would the mountain rescue people do?

He hoped Bonny would turn up quickly. 'Bonny!' His teeth rattled more as he tried to convince himself she would raise the alarm, turn back and find him. He wished he could be certain. She was capable. She really was. But he knew deep down food was always her priority. He wished he had told someone where he was going and what time he would return. The basics of fell-walking rules. 'Bonny!' It was too late now.

Light was disappearing, sleet was turning to snow, yet through a gap in the cloud he saw stars; remote observers watching his plight and they twinkled and winked in sympathy. They were swallowed by a great bank of cloud that completely enveloped him and he sobbed and blubbed prayers that were last uttered in child-hood.

Bonny reached the door of the pub and howled until it was opened. She drank water from a bowl by the bar, ate half a packet of crisps from under someone's table, she was petted and fussed before settling to sleep by the fire.

Lost Property

The steamer: Lady of the Lake, crossed paths with Raven and Fiona snapped a picture of their triangular wakes, their fans spreading wider and wider. She watched, fascinated as it was blustery on Gowbarrow yet calm on Ullswater. How could that be? The vessels glided on as she sheltered in the ruin of a former shooting lodge.

Sat beneath the lichen covered wall, she dug out her squashed sandwich and ate like she hadn't eaten for days. Tuesday was a good day for fell-walking she decided; there were few people about, except for the guy who seemed to do similar summits for a while, but he kept a respectful distance and didn't encroach on her space.

It was chilly and Fiona rummaged for a hat, but when she shifted weight, she felt something under her hand and without thinking, trailed a finger over the protruding piece. It didn't feel like stone. It didn't feel like something natural. Intrigued, she shifted to her knees and looked closely. A little piece of gold poked up from the soil and she dug out her pocket knife. Like an archaeologist who had found something precious, she made tiny, careful stabs, pushed aside brittle bracken stalks and cut away small sods. Whatever it was, it had been there a while. Walkers' boots had compacted the earth. Other people had sat in the very same spot as she, and the object was caked. She gave it a shake. It was a bracelet. It looked unloved, she decided and would take it home, give it a rinse under the tap. She recognised the type. It was a gate bracelet – like the one her gran used to wear years ago. Fiona smiled at the oft repeated story: her grandfather had bought one in a tearing hurry from Argos when he'd forgotten it was his and Gran's anniversary. He'd never lived it down. Apparently, he'd raced all the way to town on his bike, pedaling furiously no doubt, and got there two minutes before the shop shut. When he flamboyantly presented it to Gran she shoved it back saying he was a bloody cheapskate as he'd left the price ticket taped to the bottom!

The bracelet was long gone and so were her grandparents but the memory was a good one. Fiona stuffed the bracelet in her pocket and wondered how many memories were attached to the one just found. She would take it to Penrith police station later that evening – even though it was unlikely to be claimed.

Fiona put her head above the parapet and was almost blown over. The mood of the lake had changed. It was darker and white horses were rearing for a canter across its surface. It would be full steam ahead for the vessels to reach their piers. Strings of Herdies tucked in along the wall. They had the right idea. It was time for her to move, time to do the summit. The path up was sodden and Fiona squelched through boggy sedge cursing herself for wanting one more. Gowbarrow was well-known for being wet. It would be her last of the day, she vowed. The weather was closing in so fast she barely had time to pull on her waterproofs before the deluge.

The trig point had no one else on it, unsurprisingly she thought, only the hardy or head-cases would be out on a day like today. Her jacket hood flicked and flapped like the body of a kite and she pulled the cord tight. She held the bracelet to the rain and picked out bits of soggy tissue, gave it a shake and stuffed it back in her pocket. She didn't notice the man in the blue jacket until he was fifty yards away; head down but heading her way. She left the summit quickly; it wasn't the day for conversation with a stranger.

******

It was dark by 5.30 pm but Fiona could tell the police station had been there a long time. Solid, dark, a pillar of the community on the outside and no doubt a forbidding institution within. She was glad there was a light above the door, one of those old-fashioned lanterns and its swinging and creaking made her think of Sherlock Holmes. She stifled a smile and stepped into the empty room.

The hard wooden benches looked like they'd once belonged to a church or a school and the vinyl flooring had seen better days. Fiona hoped she wouldn't be there long and was grateful she got in just before someone else. The man sat with his hoodie up, face turned away from her. *Guilty!* she pronounced. And then she was called to the window.

The woman had two black lines for eyebrows and Fiona thought it was the softest thing about her. She was the seen-it-all-before type and Fiona instinctively knew the woman would prefer something more exciting than a tarnished gold bracelet being handed in. Perhaps a murder would get her juices flowing? Fiona tried to hide the silliness that was threatening to break out and get her into trouble. Clapped in iron for smiling...

'Name?'

'Fiona.'

'Surname first.' The woman barely hid her sarcasm.

'Sorry. McIntyre,' she smiled apologetically. It was lost on Sour-Cow who wouldn't meet her eye.

'Contact number?' Fiona gave it and the woman replied, 'I'll repeat that back to you's. Sign there and date it.' She jabbed her finger close to a box.

'What do you think the chances are of the owner collecting it?' Fiona's stab at conversation didn't get her anywhere and Sour-Cow shrugged before moving off. Fiona was ready to give up but ventured, 'If it's not claimed, can I have it?'

'Come back in three months.' The woman pushed a ticket towards her and slammed the glass barrier down.

Fi waited in the sandstone porch hoping for a break in the rain knowing it wasn't likely to happen. There was nothing for it but to make a run. The heavens had truly opened and The Lake District was doing its damnedest to live up to its name. She didn't care if she looked a sight with her jacket over her head – the weather was vile. Fiona stepped out and ran as fast as she dared, skidding on wet leaves and tweaking her 'bad knee' in the process. She slammed the door shut before the car seat got a soaking. 'Bollocks! That's what you get for your good deed!' Fiona gritted her teeth and rubbed at her knee. She wondered how and why people became so bloody rude and vowed she would return just so that Sour-Cow wouldn't be able to sell the bracelet on eBay.

******

Fiona was glad to be back at the cottage; she had the use of it for a long weekend and the plan was to be joined by her best friend Sarah later that evening. She looked forward to a catch-up. They vowed to do at least six Wainwright's – Eastern ones.

As she went to charge her phone, it rang and she moved closer to the window for a better signal. 'Hello? Hello? Hell-o-o?' The line went dead and Fiona looked at her screen for clues, it said: number unknown. She plugged it in and opened a bottle of beer, taking a swig as she traipsed to the lounge. Curling up in the chintz wing-chair, she became lost in TV drivel as rain lashed outside but she was content now her knee was less painful. Thirty minutes later the phone rang again and this time she raced to reach it. It stopped. Number unknown. Fiona snarled having got up through the middle of a trashy programme she couldn't believe she was watching, but before she had finished cursing and sat back – it rang again. 'Hello?' she growled.

'Hello. Miss McIntyre?' It was a man's voice. 'It's the police station.' His voice sounded muffled.

'Oh Hi! Sorry. I nearly put the phone down on you. I've had some funny calls tonight.' Fiona laughed her apologetic laugh once more and told herself to stop being so bloody subservient.

'I was just going over your paperwork and er, spilled coffee on it. We need a little more information. Where are you staying at the moment?' then added, 'I've smudged that bit.'

Fiona was amused, 'That's my trick! I spill coffee over everything! Helvellyn View. It's on the road to... erm...do you know Threlkeld? Do you know the pub – the Horse and Farrier? It's up behind there. There's only one road that goes to the Blencathra Centre. If you keep going you'll have to turn round, it's a dead end.'

'Yes. Yes. I do.'

'Well, I can't remember the name of the road, it's erm, hang on I'll get it off my paperwork.' She raced upstairs to the bedroom. At the bottom of her (almost un-packed) bag she pulled out a plastic wallet where she'd stashed the rental details, later remembering it would probably have been in the folder in the hall.

'Yes, I've got it. Sorry about that. It's...' but the line was dead. Fiona looked at her phone, curled her lip and shrugged, she decided he probably had enough information and would ring back if he needed more.

The wind was becoming fiercer and Fiona checked the forecast for the following day. Something banged down the side path and she tried looking through the single glazed window, now opaque from condensation. She wiped it with her fingers and water trickled to the sill. A light came on automatically. Fiona peered through, but still couldn't see, listened but couldn't discern anything other than the wind rattling the gutter. A wheelie-bin clattered as it dragged itself down the path. Fiona shook her head and breathed out. It was 7.15 pm and Sarah was due any moment. A car door slammed and she went to the front. The door was rustic and wooden, over-painted white, its former blue scratched through from a dog that never wanted to stay. A rectangle of frosted glass held one tiny clear diamond in the centre allowing a glimpse of outside. The security light flicked on and Fiona reached for the snib but the shadowy figure outside the door was tall. Taller than Sarah. Nevertheless, she called, 'Sarah?' She knew it wasn't her friend. All her instincts screamed don't open the door and for once she listened to the inner voice and raced to the side window where she wiped another swathe. She squinted through but the light had clicked off. A car slowed and drove on. The bin bumped and banged and the light clicked on again. The car must have turned round at the end; it was coming back. It was Sarah this time. When her engine stopped, another started and the car trickled slowly down the hill like the driver had depressed the clutch.

Fiona threw open the door and ran to greet her friend, 'Sarah! Am I glad to see you!'

'Wow! Steady on girl. It hasn't been that long!'

Fiona laughed and checked tears. 'Sorry. I've been a bit spooked tonight. Did you see someone outside the door?'

'What, just now?' Sarah opened her boot and pulled out bags.

'Yeah, some guy. I think it was a guy – as he was tall! Standing here...' she indicated with a sweep of her arm, 'when you drove past?'

'No. Sorry. What did he want?' Sarah shrugged. Fiona grabbed Sarah's hold-all and virtually dragged her friend indoors. With one hand over her mouth she paced the kitchen.

'What's up? Your eyes are huge!'

'I'm just a bit freaked out by the wind.' She waved away her friend's concern, but was clearly agitated and asked, 'Did you see a car? Did you see any cars in the road?'

'You mean here?' Sarah didn't have a clue what her friend was talking about and rolled her eyes. 'There were a few at the other cottages but I didn't take any notice. Why would I?'

Fiona let out a long breath. 'It's just that I think there was someone outside. I had some calls I'd missed earlier and then a guy from the police station rang.'

'The police rang? What have you been up to?' Sarah smirked as she pulled open her hold-all. 'Ta da! Alcohol! Sounds like you need a drink. Hey? What's the forecast like? Are we walking tomorrow or what?'

'Er. Not bad. I think this squall will clear. If it's still grotty in the morning, I might call in at the station, see what they want.'

'Have you been up to no good? You naughty girl.' Sarah obviously wasn't taking her friend seriously. Sarah had always been a tease and Fiona was grateful for the light-hearted banter and threw a close-to-hand-knitted tea-cosy in her general direction. It was expertly caught by Sarah who waggled a finger and said, 'You'll have to do better than that!'

Fiona felt better already. Sarah looked at her square-on, her curiosity piqued and asked, 'Seriously, what have you been up to? What do you need to go in for?'

'I handed in a gold bracelet.'

'Gold! I'd have kept it!'

'No you wouldn't.'

'What was it like? Worth much?'

'I dunno. I just remember my gran losing hers abroad somewhere once upon a time and thought I'd hand it in. Sentimental softy that I am.'

'Yeah, I suppose so, you were always too kind. I'd have melted it down, well you know what I mean, sent it off in one of those little jiffy bags and got twenty quid for it.'

'Mercenary cow.' Fiona tutted at her friend knowing she wasn't serious.

Sarah stretched her arms above her head before folding them and said, 'I'm starving! What are we eating tonight? Fancy a curry in Penrith? Come on let's get you out of here. We can't have you having a freaky Friday.'

'Yeah. You're on! Give me five mins.' Fiona left the kitchen watched by Sarah; she knew her limp wasn't so obvious these days but knew her friend had noticed and tried to disguise it.

******

He watched their car pass his, watched until the red lights disappeared from view. Somewhere along the line he had been told, 'If you sit very still in a car, no one ever notices you.' And tonight was pitch black. He sat for five and waited; made sure they weren't turning back for something forgotten. He was inside and up the stairs in minutes.

He opened the wardrobe, stroked a dress and softly closed it after him. A copy of Trail magazine sat on the bedside table. He snorted; she still had stupid ideas. He looked around before walking into the only other room at the top of the stairs. The floor creaked and he made a mental note. He bent his head sideways to accommodate the sloping ceiling and clicked the black latch which was stiff from too much paint. He noticed bags spilling out their contents, makeup over most of the bed, a hairbrush, a phone charger. He picked up a crumpled T-shirt and held it to his. Lucky day. Underneath was a phone which he slipped in his pocket. Back in Fiona's room he picked up a discarded pair of trousers and held them to his nose, shut his eyes and breathed deeply. 'You still smell the same delicious smell, Fi. You are all over this room.' With a misplaced reverence, he gently placed them on the bed, smoothing them out just as she'd left them. He pulled open a drawer and nodded. He'd found her underwear.

Fiona was dropped off at the cottage by Sarah who insisted on nipping back to Booths for more booze! As if they didn't have enough! She was unceremoniously dumped on the drive and shrugged. Typical Sarah! She was still muttering as she ran upstairs. It was on the top step when she caught a whiff of something familiar. Something she once knew. Fiona was no fool, as much as he knew her scent, she knew his. Like a musty coat the dog slept on, he had a particular smell. She gagged and clamped a hand tight across her mouth. Was she mistaken? Surely! She listened. All she heard was her heart banging in her ears. Yet, it reeked of him. Should she run? Run now? Or try and creep downstairs? Where was he? Was he still in the house? Surely not! There was another smell and numbly she stepped into the bedroom. Lighter fuel! It was all so quick. As realisation hit her, as that proverbial penny rolled and spun, the bedroom door slammed shut! She whirled round and was face to face with someone she never wanted to see again.

'Get out of my house!' Fiona heard her words sound rather like the headmistress she used to have at school and part of her wanted to laugh at the preposterous comment, but her belly flipped-flopped as she screamed, 'Go on! Get out now, before I call the police!'

'It's been a while Fi. Aren't you pleased to see me?' He kept his back against the door blocking her exit and fished in his pocket for a smoke. He lit a skinny roll-up without taking his eyes off her and languidly blew a smoke ring to the ceiling. 'It's been a while hasn't it?' He sucked at his crusty moustache.

Fiona weighed up her options. Was running to the window and banging on it going to attract help? Her neighbours weren't exactly close. She doubted she would be seen through the drizzle or heard over TV chatter. Should she feign interest in him? Get him to relax and drop his guard? Pretend she was pleased to see him? She chose the latter.

'Sorry. Yes, it's good to see you but you shouldn't have let yourself in.' She noticed his face become troubled and with a softer tone added, 'I see you can still blow rings. I never did get the hang of that.'

'Here. Have a drag.' He held out his arm. He smelled vile.

'No thanks. I gave up all that years ago.'

He kept his arm held out, 'Suit yourself,' took another drag, coughed and said, 'You've gone all healthy. You look fit.' He sniffed hard and looked like he was about to spit. Through glazed eyes he studied her, shook his curly hair and droplets of rain reached Fiona's face. 'Oops, I didn't realise my hair was wet.' Sarcasm was still a strong point.

'How did you find me?' Fiona forced a smile and felt her mouth twitch, willing it not to betray her.

'You were in the police station in Penrith. I overheard you when you handed in a bracelet. Four years hey? Who'd have thought it? I've been looking for you. Didn't have a clue where you were, mind. No one would tell me. The fuckers.' He coughed and smiled, 'You need to be more discreet when you give out your phone number.' Danny held his chest, his wet cough interrupting his laughter. 'Course I'd seen you earlier a couple of times. Not saying where, like. That's for me to know and you to find out.' He laughed manically having recently discovered the phrase.

Fiona nodded, unsure what to say. She had to get out but didn't have a plan for being trapped in her bedroom. Feebly, she said, 'I need the bathroom.'

'Do you, now?' Danny took another drag and looked for somewhere to stub out the smoke. Unintentionally, he dropped it. Instinctively, Fiona lurched forward to pick it up and he reacted fast.

'Not so quick, Fi.' Danny grabbed her and dragged her over to the bed. He forced her right arm close to her shoulder blades. With his mouth close to her ear he hissed, 'I only wanted to see you, you stupid bitch. I was never going to do anything!'

'Dan, for God's sake you are making this so much worse. Get off!'

'You know I've never hit a woman, you falling down the stairs was not my fault!' He licked her ear, 'That was all a big mistake. I'm not letting you go until you understand that. All of it. I'd never hurt you. I've always loved you. You know that.'

'Dan! Dan! Stop it I can hardly breathe!'

'I need you to understand. If I let you go now you will just go to the police and I can't have that. I can't go inside again.'

'Danny come on. Let go, now!' The duvet filled her face and she squirmed to get her face out of the bedding.

'Promise me you will listen! Promise! I just need to explain!'

'Okay! Okay! I will. Promise. Now just let go!'

Danny heard something crackle and kept his grip on Fiona as he glanced over his shoulder. Paper smouldered. It looked like it was about to catch but he wasn't going to let go. The paper curled. He glanced behind. It was alight. He howled in frustration and shook Fiona hard, snapping her neck like a child's. 'Tell me you will listen! Tell me!' He glanced back at the paper which was crinkling black and blue and yellow.

Danny slammed his hands between her shoulder blades, leaving a nice bruise no doubt, before making a run for it. As Fiona fought to catch her breath she lunged at the paper, stomped blackened flakes into the carpet and heard his frantic footsteps clatter down the staircase. But he didn't get further than the doorstep. Sarah had returned. Fi hadn't shut the front door and so she heard the end of the commotion. Quick as a flash she stuck out a well-placed leg and sent him nose-down into the grit. A kick in the ribs ensured he stayed there.

'Bastard!' She yelled adding another for good measure.

Fiona, framed by the doorway stood panting as she struggled for breath and said, 'Can you call the police.' She bent down to Danny and never felt stronger as she said, 'I'm not your property. I never was. And I never will be.'

'I've already rung them and I think I can hear a siren – Shit-head here,' Sarah leaned in close to him – 'you're going back Inside! For a freakin' long time! I just knew it was him when I saw the crap car parked out of sight. Smelly bastard, even his car reeks!' Sarah urged Fiona, 'Something good has to come out of this Fi...make sure you claim that bloody bracelet!'

BONUS SELECTION

The following stories are all drawn from my imagination but two in particular are inspired by a childhood spent on The Wirral. Being a peninsula, I've often thought the light is particularly good and I assume it is the proximity of the sea. It is never far away. *Ready Salted* came into being from a wistful look back across benign waters from the Greenfield area of North Wales. I had been out walking and came across a plaque telling of its links with the slave trade. It was quite a shock to discover its dark history.

Maid in Heaven also draws on my childhood based in Oxton where I met many an old character, particularly spinsters who spent a lot of time alone, rattling around big old houses, their suitors having been killed in the war. Many were, understandably, bitter and twisted—but interesting to have a biscuit with! Or maybe not.

Knowing was a lot of fun to write. I've been to quite a few garden shows over time and the fierce competition never fails to amuse. The length and breadth of Britain would understand!

Caged Bird was written as part of an anthology, set just inside North Wales. I wanted to write something that was local to the area and came up with the idea when I discovered a new prison was being built.

Ready Salted

Her appointment was at three o'clock and she found the address after much muttering and reversing of her mum's car. The sat nav was messing about and Shonice was anxious. Most of the houses were hidden from view and had large hardwood gates with intercoms and flashing LEDs warning folk to keep out, but 'The Hollies' looked untouched, unloved perhaps, yet it suited its name as the canopied entrance was dark and overgrown. Tiny ferns grew in cracks and sandstone blocks seemed pushed apart by nothing more than capillaries. She squeezed the car through over-painted iron gates which looked like they had been wedged in place since before she was born. A macabre figure sat atop a plinth, without an arm and its nose sliced off; it stared down at her in stony silence. Roses with rust-spot surrounded the courtyard's central sundial. The light no longer reached the neglected briars, but everywhere was green and most of it was mould. Her stiletto stepped onto compacted gravel and she looked up through her fringe at unblinking windows to see if anyone was watching. She could see nothing but reflected clouds. She shivered and made an effort to feel cheerful. The smell of the sea always helped and at least the weather was bright and sunny. Magnificent cedar silhouettes leaned against a cerulean sky. The house walls were painted sludge grey, once-upon-a-time shiny. It was Georgian and three storeys high, but now dull from neglect. She took a deep breath and rang the bell which was an original with circles of wood with an ivory button that said PRESS in capitals. It buzzed loud and long and she felt awkward disturbing the peace. She stepped back and waited.

'Just a minute. I'll be with you in a moment, dear.' A welcoming voice jarred with the gloom of the doorstep. A key turned and Mr. Williams said, 'Come in. Come in.' He was faster than most at offering his hand.

As expected, the interior was dark and musty but not unpleasant. Mr Williams shuffled ahead, his walking frame giving him reasonable speed as he motioned for Shonice to follow him along the panelled hall.

'Come into the morning room, it's much lighter in here. In fact it's my favourite room,' he beamed. She saw why, instantly reminded of a holiday in southern Italy, for 'The Hollies' was set high and the rear of the house had extensive views across the sea to Wales. Close to the window she could see other large houses discreetly tumbling down the hillside. It was not quite the Amalfi but on a day like today the overall impression was continental and warm, of luxury and privilege. The back of the house caught all the light and she breathed deeply, sharing the experience with the old man next to her.

'I can see you are surprised, Shonice. May I call you Shonice?' Mr Williams stood holding on to the straps of his braces as she collected her thoughts. Shonice would do. Ms Williams was too much of a coincidence. The view was breathtaking, the rear was so different from what she expected; it was a stunning space with terraced lawns that fell downhill to a sandstone wall and the patio was filled with spiky plants in over-sized terracotta pots. It was well kept, unlike the unkempt front. *To deter would-be house-breakers* was the reason he allowed it to look uncared for. Shonice wasn't sure his logic worked.

'It's very beautiful,' she said and sat where he indicated.

Mr Williams excused himself to fetch drinks. Shonice was a little alarmed that he'd parked his walking frame by the wall and watched him shuffle off. She delved into her bag for her recording equipment and checked the batteries for the second time. Shonice knew he had links with importers and exporters and knew he'd sold the company over twenty years ago but she needed to find out a lot more, for the book he would leave behind would be his tale. She needed to find out what made him tick. She had been doing the job for all of six weeks, three of which were training and she had been warned in a round-about way she would have a harder time than most to get clients to open up. Not that she needed reminding. Same old story. All the info was to be uploaded within 48 hours of the interview and she was anxious to get it right. She glanced towards the hall before delving into her bag for crisps, hoping she could scoff them before Mr Williams returned. No such luck. He caught her shovelling them in and she apologised saying she'd had no lunch. It took a while for him to deposit the tray, struggling to still his shaking and Shonice wasn't sure whether to offer help or not.

'Don't mind me, dear. I love crisps. I'm not supposed to eat them now. They interfere with my blood pressure.'

She offered one all the same and to her surprise, he took it. He managed to make one crisp last thirty seconds.

He smacked his lips. 'Lovely!' Wiping his mouth free of salt he said, 'I'll pour shall I? Mrs B left early.'

'Mrs B?'

'The lady that does for me.'

'Oh! So you live by yourself but you have help?' Shonice settled into the sofa and flicked the switch.

'Yes, I do now. I've been a widower for a number of years.' Mr Williams looked at his hands. 'Mrs Williams was taken too early.'

Shonice switched off, gave him a moment. She had been advised to pause at that point, let the interviewee recover if need be. He took a sip of his tea and laughed softly, 'She liked crisps too!' She switched back on. He was okay and in a firmer voice began his story.

'We exported copper. From over there!' He coughed, caught his breath and nodded towards the window. He meant Flint. Shonice knew the history. 'Before my time...you understand. It was certainly the start of the Williams Empire.' He snorted at his own emphasis and coughed again. 'Yes, I'm afraid we did make a lot of money from um...' He left the sentence hanging. Today was not turning out how either of them expected. Slavery was a topic best left in the past.

******

Her second visit was two weeks later and it took a while to settle into the interview as Mrs B traipsed back and forth with the vacuum. She clattered and clanged: ostensibly baking a cake, the mixer whizzing on and off at regular intervals. Every now and then she peered over her spectacles at Shonice who didn't find it difficult to read her mind. Marked as a thief for her colour. Shonice was used to it and could put people down with a sentence. Her accent could stop them in their tracks. It was never what they expected. She chuckled softly and covered it with a cough, it was a good job her initial interview was over the phone or she'd never have landed the job. Never in a million years. The simple Mrs B was presented with Shonice's winning smile. Why bother winding her up? It was met with a renewed flurry of whisking activity and Shonice hid her grin behind her hand.

'She won't be long, dear.' Mr Williams patted her arm and nodded to where the noise was coming from.

Shonice stopped recording and reached for a biscuit dislodging the paper doily and self-consciously nudged it back.

'I do like a nibble. They're good aren't they?' Mr Williams said as he crunched, pretending he hadn't seen the exchange.

They were good. Thomas Williams was her last appointment of the day and Shonice looked at her watch. It was only two o'clock and she could stay a bit longer; Lifetime Books didn't have many clients and she could take her time. They chatted about the weather and how the peninsula caught the Gulf Stream, how the water flowed from warmer climes. They talked about the palms and why they could survive there, but not 39 miles inland. Shonice waited as Mrs B squeezed into her coat and suppressed a smile knowing she was still being watched with suspicion.

When Mrs B pulled the door after her, Shonice rummaged in her bag, 'I know you said you shouldn't eat these but I've brought you some crisps,' she peeled off the lid and held out the box and waited. 'I made them myself. There is salt on them though. Sorry about that, it's just a habit of mine to sprinkle it all over.' Flustered, she carried on, 'They don't taste the same without. My mum showed me how to make them. She was taught by her mother in Jamaica...'

Mr Williams shifted in his seat and reached for another. 'They are rather good. Lovely.' He took another and they carried on eating. The crunching was loud and filled the room. It was easier than talking. Shonice thought about ringing Lifetime Books and backing out, it was all so awkward, but she needed the money before returning to uni.

'What are you studying?' he asked.

'Law and history.'

'Oh. That sounds intriguing. Tell me more.'

She told him a little about her life, waffled on about her grandparents' market stall and her mum's clothes shops. Some of it was easy but she hit a brick wall and both were further embarrassed. She knew why she wanted to delve into the past but hadn't expected the past to slap her in the face whilst doing the part-time job. It hadn't occurred to her that her distant past would race into her future, yet she could forgive him, couldn't she? Couldn't she forgive them all? She was aware time forever marched on, yet the house held to its past with a tenacity she could feel in its very walls.

Unable to breathe she needed to leave, needed to get out and snatched up her Tupperware box and sweet potato crumbs floated to the floor. She'd learned enough about his hardware chain. Chains for him and chains for them. She was not going to return. Stuff the money. And yet, not eighteen months later she was back there. Alone. Mr Williams had left her The Hollies.

Maid in Heaven

The bell on the wall jangled. It paused before jiggling insistently like the world would end if it wasn't answered immediately. It couldn't be ignored. She'd tried. Enid sighed and watched the little metal bell work itself into an apoplectic fit. It was time to take tea up to the ladies. 'There's no rest for the wicked,' she said to herself, 'and I must be very wicked 'cos I'm not getting any rest what-so-ever!' She knew she was two minutes late and hurriedly prepared cups, saucers and plates and placed them with their handles pointing the same way as instructed. She straightened hand-stitched cloth so it overlapped the tray an inch on each side. Exactly. Enid frowned on spotting a stain and hastily covered it with the cake stand, hoping the sisters wouldn't notice.

Teaspoons were inspected and breathed, huffed and puffed upon, polished with her apron. They would just about pass muster. 'They'd have my guts for garters if they didn't gleam.' Enid was used to talking to herself and chuckled as she hummed a tune from long ago. A doily was placed on the best floral china, slices of sticky fruit cake were arranged in a fan and delicately overlapped by half an inch. Cherries glistened. Rich, dark nuts asked to be picked. She closed her eyes and inhaled deeply. That was all she would be allowed. A sniff. It wasn't worth pinching a slice as the sisters would know.

The bell jiggled a third time, more insistently and Enid knew if she wasn't up the stairs within thirty seconds, there would be trouble. She would be for it!

'Sorry, Miss.' Enid bobbed before placing the laden tray on a side table. Her apology was not acknowledged. She was invisible. Always was. She often felt like a ghost slipping silently between rooms, barely leaving a trace. The sitting room was still and silent, save for the 'dook, dook' of the mantle clock. Matching leather chairs faced away from her and only the wisps of greying locks was all that told her the seats were occupied.

The room was stuffy. Drapes at the long windows were in want of taking down and beating but being the last of the staff, there was never enough time for all the chores. Never enough time to catch up. Enid took a step towards the window and reached for the cord to let in a little more light, but she froze as Hester's voice pierced the silence.

'Don't touch that!'

Enid held her breath and waited until the creak of Hester's chair told her Hester was easing back, easing into her plump upholstered wing, and back into her sanctum. Enid stood stock still, waited for the second creak knowing the chair would sigh and settle. And when she heard the little noise that sounded like a snore that wasn't a snore, she knew a satisfied smile would be in place and ten seconds more meant Hester's eyes would close.

Enid took a step backwards and spotted a beam of dust motes cutting diagonally across the room. Hanging like a wand, particles twirled and danced and she had an overwhelming desire to put her hand through it, freeze the moment just to see if it held any magic for her.

'That will be all for now, Girl.'

'Yes, Miss.' Enid backed out and closed the door as quietly as possible after her, the turn of the handle reminding her she was on the outside. Always would be.

Enid knew the twins were getting tetchier by the day, but she understood them. They were sad old biddies. Neither had ever had a suitor, not as far as she knew. It was such a shame really. Most of the local men had been claimed by the war. There were no men left. Dusty jars, that's all they were. Been left on the shelf too long. But, at least she was young; Enid shrugged and hoped that she might still meet someone who would care for her and casting off the sisters' shadow she hitched up her skirt, threw a leg over the banister and whooshed down the lavender waxed handrail to the kitchen.

******

Enid held the bed covers to her neck. It was freezing. The room was still black and she knew there was ice on the inside of the window. The pokey attic struggled to hold any heat–not helped by the fact a pane of glass had a small crack in it for as long as Enid could remember! Every now and then she blocked the little hole with scrunched up paper. Tentatively, she dared put an arm outside the covers and withdrew it fast.

'Blimey! It's ruddy Arctic and won't help my chilblains one jot!' As ever, she laughed at herself and after a count of three, flung the bedsheets aside and snatched at her stockings. She cursed the cold once more and dithered as her flesh goose-pimpled. Her fingers poked through the same holes that were mended more times than she cared to remember. Enid growled knowing she needed to pull her finger out if she was going to be on time this morning.

It was barely light, but fires had to be lit and water had to be heated. Hortensia was a grumpy beggar at the best of times.

'Mornin' Miss.' Enid carried the scalding pitcher to the washstand and placed it so the handle was out of harm's way. She drew the curtains aside and a muffled, vexatious rumble issued from the lump that was still curled up under the eiderdown.

Enid, placing one foot behind the other, backed out and raced downstairs two at a time, avoiding the treacherous loose stair rod–when she wanted to be quick her feet were faster than the banister! A second jug of water was needed, this time for Hester.

As she waited for the boil, she heard a long, gurgling scream of what could only be described as blind fury. It was swiftly followed by a second, longer scream of enraged indignation. Enid didn't move. She thought the screech came from Hortensia's room. But she couldn't move. Her brain said, 'shift yourself' but her legs wouldn't budge. There was panic. Feet ran – but they weren't hers!

Hester bellowed, "What has that stupid girl done now?"

Enid felt her eyes ready to pop. She could feel them about to burst! Round and black, her brother used to tease her. 'Alley-eyes! Alley-eyes!' and she would hurl fistfuls of marbles in his direction. They usually missed. She knew she had 'Alley-eyes' right now.

The sisters were running downstairs, racing towards the kitchen. They never normally came downstairs. It meant only one thing. Trouble.

'Get some water!' Hortensia screamed. 'No, no, no! Cold! You imbecile!' Hortensia had obviously tipped the pitcher of water over herself; her nightgown was drenched from neck to waist. Enid was drawn to the blistering arm. 'Turn on the tap, you idiot girl! Look what you've done!'

Enid turned the tap as far as it would go, the pipe banged and rattled against the wall as a torrent gushed and spattered Hortensia's night robe some more. Hortensia did not relish water.

Enid soaked a cloth, wringed it and wrapped it around Hortensia's chubby arm. She heard herself apologising over and over knowing she wasn't heard, knowing she wasn't being listened to and was unsure why she was to blame. But, Hortensia's glare told her somehow she must be. Enid gently peeled away the cloth and replaced it with another whilst Hortensia keened, rocking backwards and forwards. Her moans were the oddest sound Enid had heard.

'My arm is ruined! Ruined! Look what your carelessness has done! I've instructed you on the art of getting things right! Time after time I've worked with you. This just isn't good enough!'

'I did place the handle towards the back Miss, I...'

'How dare you interrupt? Such impudence! Go to your room! Go! Go! Immediately!' Hortensia pointed at the door, her face wormed with ugliness. 'Go! You stupid, stupid girl! I'm ruined!'

Enid ran. Fought the urge to vomit and paced her floor until she could pace no more. She flung herself on the bed and curled up. With hands clamped tightly over ears she sang, *All things bright and beautiful*. Until the silence came.

******

It was hours later when Enid crept into the hall in the hope of discerning any movement or sound from the sisters. The house was too quiet. As she crept further out, the creak of the wooden floor gave her away and she bit her fingers. With head cocked, she listened over the banister, but heard nothing. The house was as silent as the Chapel on Monday. Lamps hadn't yet been switched on. It was time to make the usual tea-tray but Enid wasn't sure today was a usual day. There was nothing for it; life had to go on and she put her nose in the air and took the banister route to the basement.

Which sister first spoke, first spat the word she did not know but the word chilled her even though she didn't understand what the word meant.

'Retribution.' they said in unison. 'There – will – be – retribution.'

******

The house became quieter than she'd ever known before. The bell jangled less and less over the next 48 hours. The sisters fell silent but she knew when she was out of earshot they were discussing things. Discussing her.

Enid rifled the shelves for the dictionary that had once lurked in the hallway and eventually found it but her recall of the word she'd heard and her lack of spelling capacity made it a fruitless search and she replaced the dictionary back on the shelf.

It wasn't long before she had an idea of what the word meant. She was sent to look for something in the cellar which was never a place she enjoyed visiting—the spiders were the size of cats and the rats even bigger! It was when she was almost at the bottom of the staircase that the door slammed shut. And the key turned in the lock. Enid heard the sisters' footsteps walking away. They weren't hurried. They were steady, deliberate steps. Instinctively she knew it was wise not to shout out and hugged herself tightly. A whimper escaped her lips, 'Please...' Her word reached no one.

The beams above were weighted with filthy cobwebs and Enid pulled her cap firmly over her ears and tried not to look upwards. She knew she would have to sit it out. Perhaps they just needed to teach her a lesson? They just needed someone to blame? It wasn't very warm down here. Dank and darkly shadowed she didn't want to look too closely in the black corners where surely the rats scurried? Enid swallowed and thought if she stayed put on the top step, stayed exactly where she was she would be okay. She would manage for half an hour– or so! When she heard footsteps return, her spirits leapt but to her horror the light was switched off and the dark gripped. Tight.

'No! Please! Let me out!' Enid felt for the handle and banged and banged on the panelled door. 'Please, please let me out. I'm sorry! It was an accident. I'm really sorry!' She hammered away. 'Please, please come back!' She hammered until her hand hurt. 'Please, please don't leave me in here. Miss Hortensia?'

Enid slumped and fought the urge to cry. Her mind raced with myriad thoughts and she knew she would get out sooner if she kept quiet, kept calm. After what seemed like half an hour–although time was difficult to gauge–she stood and knocked calmly, 'Hello? Can you hear me? I'm very cold. Hello? Are you there? I need to tend the fires for you. I have to cook for you soon. Hello? Miss Hester?'

'Turn the gramophone off. I'm sick of listening to it,' Hortensia waved her good arm towards her sister; 'I think she's shut up now anyway.'

Hester glared at her older twin and stubbornly refused to move instantly just to please her. After a considered length of time in which Hortensia sighed repeatedly, Hester rose and opened the lid of the cabinet. The 78 spun. Its crackle hic-cupped.

'Oh, stop being so utterly selfish and lift that blasted handle will you?'

Hortensia's glare was having no effect on Hester. Needling her sister was one thing Hester was very good at and she turned and said, 'Do you think she's had enough? Or do you think we should leave her a bit longer?' Hester twiddled her hair, a habit since childhood, something she did when she couldn't make up her mind. 'I don't know...perhaps we should put the light back on?'

'I think we should let her out, it's freezing in here. She'll have enough to catch up with, that'll be sport enough don't you think? Besides she's probably better at tending my arm than you are. Go and unlock the door!'

'Hmm, maybe another ten minutes. Let's put some more music on shall we?'

******

When the door was finally unlocked and Enid stumbled into the hall, she was numb with cold. She straightened her cap and touched her face where the imprint of the wood she had been leaning on had patterned her features. Which sister opened the door, she wasn't sure but her mumblings of gratitude fell on deaf ears. Warmth and food were a priority, but a command cut through her hotch-potch of thoughts.

'Look sharp! The house is cold, get the fires lit.'

******

Enid was extra careful each time she carried water to the sisters' rooms and couldn't help comment when placing handles to the rear, 'There Miss, I've turned the jug away so you won't catch yourself.' She would bob and back out of the room quickly knowing her presence irked The Bed Blobs as she often thought of them. It made her giggle. Her thoughts were something she could own. Something no one could take from her and that cheered her no end. Enid hitched her skirt up and whooshed to the basement. She'd clawed back time enough for a much needed cuppa and with an exaggerated flop nestled into the cushions on Mr Barnsley's old chair.

******

Life went on much the same for approximately two weeks but a smashed plate was enough to tip the sisters into a frenzy and she was once again led to the cellar with the crones gripping her on each side. Of course she protested. Of course she screamed. But there was no one to hear her as the ochre scratched door was pushed aside and her body propelled forward by a fist in the small of her back. The light went off but after a couple of minutes it flickered and dimmed and to her delight stayed on. Small mercies she thought, grateful for dodgy electrics.

Enid yelled for effect. It was expected of her. She knew without a shadow of a doubt it pleased the sisters to hear her distress. Every few minutes she would call out and bang on the door. The music was turned up. The haunting strains of The Very Thought of You floated down to the cellar. Enid half-smiled at the irony. It was cold but at least she was having a rest.

She must have been down there well over an hour and she was not only cold, she was bored. The horrors of the cellar still lurked but had receded a little with familiarity and the forethought to hide an old blanket had helped somewhat. She pulled it up around her neck, gave another plaintive yell expecting to be in there a while longer but this time heard feet coming towards her and she stuffed the blanket behind a tea-chest and took on the demeanour of someone subdued.

******

On the following Sunday, on her half-day off, after church, Enid took a surreptitious stroll around the garden. She knew it was frowned upon but she didn't care today, she felt good. She wasn't due in for half an hour and sat on a slatted bench hidden by overgrown laurel and yew and tilted her face to the weak March sunlight. The world was changing and she wondered if she could perhaps work elsewhere one day? Perhaps move to a different place and be a shop-girl? It was all the rage now. People were moving on. Things were altering for girls like her. There were newer freedoms to be had. And once the thought of changing her life had gripped her, she could think of nothing else. The sunshine was good and she leaned backwards intending to rest against the wall but lost her balance.

'Goodness. I'm such a clumsy oaf!' Enid adjusted her hat and dusted her coat free of mould as she whispered, 'I really shouldn't talk to myself so much. Especially if I'm going to be a shop-girl!' She knew her time outside was short and was grateful she couldn't be seen from the windows but as she looked up, she realised there was something perplexing about the wall, something very odd about the brickwork that didn't add up and she wasn't sure why until she pushed aside the over-growth. It revealed an archway with a window. It was grimed, green and earth was half-way up it – covered in last year's weeds and leaf mould. She spat on her handkerchief and wiped a small pane, a circle of roughly six inches and put her eye to it. To her great disappointment it was blanked-off, shuttered, blocked in some way but Enid had registered a potential escape route from the cellar. It would be fun investigating. With a lighter heart she 'plumped' the laurel back into place and skipped to the rear porch ready for duty.

******

When Enid found five spare minutes, she ran to the cellar and took with her a few small items which would ensure her next incarceration would be easier. She hid an oil lamp and a tin containing a few biscuits. Progressively, she pushed aside years of accumulated rubbish in her search for the window. It wasn't an easy task; the cellar was more of a dumping ground and just in case the sisters ventured that way, she put everything back that she'd moved. Enid had a very good idea of where the window would be as the outside was echoed by arches inside. Three of them, but only the middle one held the promise of a window. When she glimpsed the frame, she clapped her hands, barely able to contain her excitement. Ironically, she wanted to stay in the cellar, but knew she'd been down there long enough and so with skirts gathered, raced back to the kitchen.

As Enid rolled pastry, she realised she was happier than she'd been for a while. The prospect of the cellar was becoming less of a fear, more a place of refuge. Even the rats weren't so frightening and she hesitated about putting down the poisoned batch of biscuits. She felt a bit sorry for them and so decided she would keep the baited tin out of sight, right at the back of the pantry until needed. They were there if she changed her mind.

In anticipation of her next detention, she increased her food stash and checked the hidden lamp, making sure it had enough oil as the sisters selfishly insisted she hand over the pathetic single bulb that once provided a little dim light.

******

The gramophone crackled into life and Hortensia leaned forward from her chair.

'This is becoming too much of a habit don't you think? It's far too much of an inconvenience having the girl in the cellar with this monotonous regularity. We end up having tea far later than usual and having to tend fires ourselves. What do you think the solution is?' Hortensia waited for a response but Hester was on her feet, swaying in time to Al Bowlly. 'Are you listening to me? Oh for goodness sakes, turn that down and open your eyes! I can hardly hear myself speak!'

'What?' Hester cupped her hand to her ear but she knew exactly what Hortensia had said.

'I said...'

Hester turned the music off, interrupting with, 'There's no need to shout. I heard. I don't know what the answer is. Maybe we should replace her? Get someone else?'

Hortensia snorted, 'That would be impossible given our location. Everyone has drifted to the larger towns. I don't know what the answer is. Other than making our point a bit stronger.'

'What do you mean?'

'Reminding her of how she came to be here in the first place and how difficult it is to get work without a reference. Ungrateful wench.' Hortensia fiddled with her ear. 'Maybe we should teach her a lesson?'

'And do what?'

'I don't know...but we need to get this sorted. One way or another. In fact I'm going to go down there and sort it right now! Remind her, if she doesn't pull her socks up, there will be consequences.'

Hortensia pushed her sleeves up to her elbows and left the room faster than the stuffed gazelle on the chimney breast once ran. Hester followed, stumbling on the hall runner. It was Enid's stupid fault for putting too much polish on the floor. The wretched girl had to go.

******

The sisters, united in anger, waited for Enid to come up from the cellar and enter the hall.

'Hurry up! We haven't got all day!' The sisters said, almost in perfect unison. Hortensia banged her stick on the open cellar door and stood back, adjusted her skirt and waited. She held her head erect, displaying a livid turkey neck; she was ready to peck.

Hester's foot twitched, she couldn't hold it in trip position for much longer and yelled into the void, 'Get here now Enid and I mean NOW!' But Hester was first to realise that something was different. Something didn't add up. Everyone knew the cellar was a cold place but the draught that blew towards them was a blast fresh from Siberia! She peered into the gloom and said, 'The window!'

Hester reached the bottom of the steps in time to see Enid's bottom shuffling in an effort to get her leg up and through the gap that was barely big enough for a child to squeeze through. As Hester lunged past tea-chests to grab Enid's ankle, her skirt hooked the lamp and it crashed on the hard brick floor spattering oil everywhere. A blue flame popped and ignited but Hortensia, whippet-fast, snatched at a discarded blanket and smothered her sister. When they pulled apart from their strangest embrace, Enid was gone.

******

Hester directed Samuel Mason to the cellar and instructed him to brick up the window. He suggested he use bricks from the floor and utilise them as they were the same type as the walls. After an uneasy negotiating process—Hester normally didn't do these things—they eventually agreed a price. Samuel emphasised how busy he was and how lucky they were to have him. He was in demand. Men were. He agreed to organising the delivery of mortar from Simpson's as he knew how much was needed and it would speed up the process. Mason, a short, stocky man, left abruptly, barely tapping his hat as courtesy. Hester knew she had capitulated on the financial aspect but tomorrow the window-gap would be filled.

******

Hester festered and fidgeted. Hortensia grumbled and growled. Since Enid had gone, (it had been over a week now) they'd had to do for themselves and learning to fetch and carry was beneath them. Their only bonus was they became fitter as they lost weight.

'Let's listen to the wireless. There might be something interesting on tonight,' Hester suggested, 'I'm fed up of hearing that howling wind and rain.'

Hortensia looked over the top of her spectacles and Hester took it for agreement, but before Hester reached the dial, there was a rap on the front door. It was late, it was dark and they never had visitors. Neither moved, both stood staring at each other understanding nothing. There was another louder rap and the sisters, one behind the other, sidled along the hallway. The vestibule was in darkness, having no one to change the blown bulb.

The porch framed two silhouettes, one broad, one thin and the sisters knew, yet opened the door only slightly. The last of the dry leaves whipped themselves into a frenzy around their ankles. Branches creaked, black twigs flew and Hortensia hit by the strength of the wind was too stunned to speak and waved them indoors.

The constable stepped forward. 'Evening Ladies. Look who I found wandering about.' PC Bampot pushed Enid forward, propelling her into the hallway where she dripped onto the tiles. Enid heard the sisters' sharp intake of breath and was glad she couldn't see their features. 'Now I'm not one to judge, but she's done you wrong Misses Henchurch and she knows that, but go kindly. She's no doubt starving. Some dry clothes and start again in the morning I'd say. You can discuss what's what tomorrow. I know you are relieved she's back. I said she wouldn't go far, not having family. I'll look in again soon,' he added, 'the cellar is not the best place for a young woman when she has done wrong, so go-easy on her.' Goodnight Misses Henchurch.' He tapped his helmet in salute. 'Goodnight.'

Hortensia shut the door, momentarily leaning against it before putting the chain across. She pointed towards the staircase and almost without emotion said, 'Go to your room, get changed and be quick!' And word for word they said together, 'It's almost time for dinner.'

Hester opened and shut her mouth three times as she tugged at her sister's sleeve, dragging her into the sitting room. They could barely contain their glee.

'Well! What a turn up for the book! We can eat properly for tonight! Thank goodness the girl is back!' Hortensia sniggered, 'She won't get out of that cellar now!'

******

Time passed and Enid kept her head down. She knew she would be 'punished' at some stage but had no illusions as far as escape was concerned. When summoned for the anticipated lecture on escaping, the sisters watched her face closely for a reaction when they told her about the window alterations. Enid stared fixedly at the threadbare carpet, determined yet passive, as Hortensia addressed her. It was obvious she could barely hide her contempt, 'Mr Mason helped us out just over a week ago, so don't get any stupid ideas Enid. It's all bricked up now.' Enid heard her lick her lips.

It was later that evening when much to Enid's surprise, Hester visited her in the kitchen and asked for tea and biscuits. Enid knew the sisters must have helped themselves whilst she was away and perhaps venturing to the kitchen had become a late-night habit? Hester further surprised her when she asked, 'Where did you go—when you were away?'

'Not far, Miss.'

'Where did you stay?' she asked, and softened it by, 'we were concerned for your safety.'

Enid smiled briefly, not believing what she had heard. 'I slept in a barn. Up near Todd's.' She nodded a direction towards the front of the house and Hester kept quiet, obliging her to add more. 'I didn't have much food. I didn't steal it. I just saved it up. I'm sorry Miss.'

'Well, you won't be trying that again, I take it. Goodnight, Enid.'

'Goodnight, Miss.'

Enid wasn't fooled by the apparent kindness of Hester. She knew, if she ever escaped again, they would know where to look! Not that there was any chance now. Her only opportunity would be to gain a job somewhere but she would have to plan meticulously, keep her eyes and ears open for anything available. Not for the first time did she wish she had family to call on and ask their advice but she was determined her life would move on. Meanwhile, a little planning was needed and with a wry smile she stole down to the cellar and hid a few items.

Enid pulled her cardigan tight about her. The cellar was, for the main part, just the same but the area beneath the window had been cleared where Mr. Mason had worked. He'd left the cement, lime and a small stack of bricks behind. The floor held a neat oblong where the bricks had been taken up and Enid shuddered before running upstairs. It was late and she needed sleep.

******

The fires were lit, muffins were made; kedgeree was next on her list. Today was a special day. It was the sisters' birthday. Enid had no idea how old they were and didn't care much to find out, but she knew the sisters would be expecting a decent spread and set-to in preparation.

The sisters would place great importance on having treats but it would be at the expense of the usual chores. It would take a week to catch up. The clock struck the hour and Enid bit her nails knowing she was behind already and stepped up the pace. Being exhausted by 10am was out of the question. By 3pm she teetered into the sitting room carrying a fully laden tray. And that's when she tripped and all hell was let loose. The fire hissed its betrayal. Specks of hot water evaporated and steam curled up the chimney. The rug was spattered with Spode and Enid picked herself up from the floor knowing everything was ruined. Nothing would be the same again. The biddies were on their feet. Hortensia and Hester shouted from above her. Mouths moved. Eyes bulged.

'You can't be trusted to do such a thing! What on earth has got into you? If you can't carry a simple thing such as a tray, you are of no use to us! We warned you!'

Enid knew a thousand words escaped their lips yet curiously heard nothing. Their faces distorted into over-blown fury. Noise washed over her as each sister clasped an arm and dragged her toward the hall. Enid glanced at her spattered apron. All her efforts, all her work–wasted. The sisters continued shouting but Enid heard nothing until she realised their fingernails were piercing her skin.

'I'm not going in the cellar!' She halted, dug her heels into the floor and tried to wriggle free. She wanted to pull off her cap and thrown it down. 'I'm not going in the cellar! I'm giving you my notice. I'm finished here! It was all an accident! Let go!' But the podgy hands were surprisingly strong.

As she wrestled, Hester pushed the cellar door with her foot and it banged against the wall, almost closing again but Hester was quick and caught it with her arm. 'Get in there and calm down you stupid, stupid girl.' Enid was shoved in backwards. The door was shut. They heard the fall. The moan. And walked away.

The gramophone went on. Louder than usual and Hortensia and Hester stuffed the remains of cake into their mouths. The vicar came and went and the sisters were grateful Enid had kept quiet.

'She's playing a trick. Thinks she will get out faster if she makes less noise. I tell you...the girl isn't coming out tonight!' Hortensia said what she wanted and sat back in her chair.

'Do you think so? I'm going to go down to the kitchen. I'm still hungry. Those biscuits are quite more-ish don't you think? Yes, maybe she should stay in overnight? What a fiasco with the tray. On our birthday too! Stupid girl.'

Hester searched every cupboard, ignoring the half prepared food Enid had been in the middle of preparing and eventually found what she was looking for. As she left the kitchen she cocked her head towards the cellar. There wasn't a sound.

'I've found some! Do you want one?' Hester held the tin towards her sister.

'No, I don't. I'll have some more of that cake. Cut me a slice will you?'

Hester decided not to take issue and said, 'You'll have to get it yourself from the kitchen. We've eaten the last piece up here.'

'Oh be a dear, Hester and get some for your older sister will you?' Hortensia turned on her most charming smile, 'You know where to look. You know I hate going below stairs. Oh go on!'

'Oh for goodness sakes, Horti you have legs!' Hester growled, 'Mother said it was two minutes' difference between us. It doesn't entitle you to a lifetime of me being...' Hester muttered making her way out of the room.

'Here. Cake as requested.' When seated, she said, 'I do think the girl is a bit quiet. She hasn't made a sound all evening. I had a listen at the door, but...nothing.'

Hortensia snorted, 'If she thinks we'll fall for her tricks, she has another think coming. Put the wireless on.'

'Mmm, I suppose you could be right. Do you know, these biscuits are heavenly!' Hester scoffed the last three and stretched out before the dying fire where they dozed until it became chilly.

After an hour of doing nothing, Hortensia stirred first and said, 'Go and let her out. I need my bed warmed. 'Go on. Don't look at me like that. You'll be quicker!'

Hester scowled and left.

******

Hortensia heard her sister's shriek from two floors up. It chilled her and she knew, but sat waiting until she heard a second, louder shriek. She watched the door, heard her sister's footsteps running towards it and when it opened and Hester couldn't spit the words out, she knew for certain.

'She's, she's...' Hester shook her head, 'She's dead!'

Hortensia rose, walked calmly towards her and placed a hand on her shoulder. Hester's pallor and terrified eyes told her everything, yet she asked, 'Are you certain?'

'Of course I'm certain! What do you take me for? The girl is dead! What are we going to do? I said she was quiet didn't I? We are going to be in so much trouble! She tripped didn't she? I'm sure she did. Oh Horti whatever will we do?'

Hortensia swallowed, rubbed her hand across her mouth, her eyes darted left and right. 'She died in the cellar she loved so much. She can stay in the cellar. Mason took up enough bricks. She can go in the hole. We have enough lime, cement, whatever to patch it up. No one will ever suspect...' Hortensia thought aloud, 'The cellar needed tidying up anyway. She has...had a reputation for going missing. We will have to stick to our plan.'

Hester was incredulous. 'You mean to say you would bury the poor girl in our cellar without a proper service or anything? Oh come on Horti this is preposterous. We'll never get away with it!'

Hortensia noted her sister's shaking, 'Get a grip for goodness sakes; we will be responsible for this girl's death unless we do something about it. And quickly! Do you want to go to prison? Do you want everything splashed over the Gazette? Because mark my words, we will lose everything. We cannot risk it being an accident–which of course it was! We must act. Tonight!'

******

It was some days later when PC Bampot knocked on the door of Orchard House to see if everything was all right. It had been noted Enid was not in church.

'Oh the silly girl has gone missing again.' Hortensia explained on the doorstep.

'She left a few days ago. Thursday I think.' She dismissed him with a wave of her hand.

'I see,' said Bampot, not fully comprehending. He took a step towards the sisters who had no intention of letting him in. 'I'd like to establish if she has taken anything. If that's convenient?' Bampot waited, saw the exchange between the sisters.

Hortensia and Hester, taken aback, allowed him through, realising they hadn't thought of clearing Enid's bedroom and said, 'Her belongings are still here. Clearly she intends returning.' Hortensia bluffed, 'Not that we will be pleased, but we could do with a little help. In the meantime if you know of anyone...'

Bampot pursed his lips, 'You say Thursday?' and licked the end of his pencil ready to make notes. 'In that case you won't mind if I take a look around?' He stepped in.

The sisters acquiesced and moved aside, all the while watching as the Constable trailed his finger along the well-polished hand-rail as he trod softly up to the top floor. Hortensia prodded her sister in the ribs and hissed, 'Hold your nerve will you!' Hester thought she was going to be sick and was visibly shaking. Hortensia thought of slapping her but was interrupted by the PC.

'I'd like to see the cellar too!'

'Mr Bampot, that was quick! You startled me! Certainly! It's this way...' Hortensia led and looked over her shoulder at him, 'but there is nothing of interest down here.' She held the door before following him down. Hester with her knuckles stuffed in her mouth, peered from the top of the stairs.

'I see.' He strode around the tea-chests, fascinated by the changes to the floor.

Hortensia tried to divert his thinking, 'You can see where Mason bricked up the window. He took the bricks from here – it left a bit of a hole, so it needed patching up afterwards, hence the new work.' Hester willed her sister to shut up.

'Mason must have been in a hurry to finish. That – or he'd had a drink.' Hester tittered. Bampot twirled his moustache, 'Never mind,' he looked up, 'I'll have a word with him. Standards are slipping.' He watched Hortensia closely, hoped for a reaction but didn't get one; she was too busy watching her sister and he wondered why. He wasn't done; he needed more information and hinted at a cup of tea which the sisters were only too quick to provide.

PC Bampot noted their demeanour as they scurried around the kitchen with an ineptitude he hadn't seen in a long time. Clearly, they were used to Enid doing everything and he suppressed a smile as Hester opened cupboards and drawers on the hunt for biscuits. Things were not fitting back in their usual places and tins and trays clattered to the floor. Hortensia used both hands to lift the kettle into place. It looked like she'd put in far too much water.

'Found some! The girl has a tin hidden at the back of the cupboard. Probably kept them for herself. She did silly things like that. Please...do have some. We can sit upstairs if you prefer..?' Hester bobbed as she pushed the tin towards him and said to her sister, 'Gosh Horti, the water is taking a long time to boil!'

'I'm perfectly happy to have tea here. Thank you, ladies.' Bampot drew himself up to his full height which was only just taller than Hortensia. The sisters stood alongside each other at the sink, kept their backs to him but he couldn't fail to notice more exchanged glances. There was something that wasn't right, something that didn't add up and he would get to the bottom of it...after another biscuit.

'Oh!' The sisters stopped and looked at each other. 'Oh Goodness!' they said in unison.

'Well, I think there is someone at your door. Perhaps you had better answer it. It could be the girl.' Bampot watched the motionless sisters. He was not going to offer to open it for them. Hortensia reached for the tea-towel, dried her hands. Hester smoothed her skirt, patted her hair and she glided towards the door.

Bampot listened, sneaked another couple of biscuits, it was probably a trader.

Movement was heard on the floor above; Bampot narrowed his eyes and scanned the kitchen, noticing the clock hadn't been wound. It had stopped at ten to three. He headed towards the voices.

Hortensia's skirt swished as she swept into the hall. She said it was no one in particular. After a polite exchange and a little joke about Mason's cellar-improvements, Bampot said he would take a look around the garden before reporting back to the station. There was another look between the sisters and he took a little pleasure watching their eyes grow larger when he said he would return.

He let himself out into the back garden and wandered down the remnants of a path. Old mistletoe and ivy tapped him on his shoulders. He turned round and caught sight of a curtain twitch.

There must have been two acres to the house; it had been a fine garden in its hey-day. His boots glistened and squeaked as he sauntered on sodden grass. This end of the garden hadn't been touched for years. He spotted something. A tucked-away shed that looked like it was ready to collapse, looked like it would take a finger to push it over. He tried the door, noting its aged hasp and padlock and gave it a shove, but to his surprise nothing budged. His hands were now covered in green slime and he wiped them on the dew. As he straightened, he realised he was light-headed. The lop-sided shed was beginning to look more lop-sided. It needed demolishing but he was curious and staggered round the back of it, perhaps see if there was a window. A wave of nausea swept over him and he put a hand out to steady himself. In slow motion Bampot dropped to his knees, sweat trickled down his chin and he fell, face down into the remnants of last year's nettles.

Knowing

The night before had been frantic. Mother made us a casserole and had used Bertie's onions! I was demented. I couldn't speak for ten minutes. Mother's brain is cabbaged these days and there was no point in trying to explain why I was standing over her, tearing my hair out. The casserole was plated up and I forced myself to eat. I had to. They were Bertie's last. It didn't taste any different from usual. I could have wept. It was my own fault for leaving them there, but as I choked down a carrot, I had an idea. Mother was still rabbiting on about putting another Oxo cube in for flavour when I ran out, saying I needed to do something.

The shed at the bottom of the garden was kept closed by a combination lock and I fiddled with it in panic. I just couldn't get the thing open. Intermittent blobs of rain were threatening to turn into a downpour; they were already soaking my blouse and I ran back to the porch. 'Mother, what's the code for the shed?' I hollered at her. It was unfair, she didn't know. I yanked open the drawer that held all the kitchen rubbish. The code was written down on the back of a packet of Duracell.

6234 6234. I don't know why it escaped me and I don't know why I thought it was a good idea to look in the shed – I knew all the boxes were empty. In my grief, I'd given away all I could, but I still needed to look. I stepped inside. It reeked of him. Bertie was so organised, everything was neat and tidy. I pulled boxes from the top shelves, hoping I'd missed something, yet nothing but dry peat floated onto my shoulders. As I brushed it off, it turned into muddy streaks. Not my best look, I'm afraid. I ran in and changed my blouse before a mad supermarket sweep ensued. I needed onions. I visited four different supermarkets before finding something that would do. Waitrose saved the day!

******

I turned the key and let myself into our local village hall and was immediately hit by the pong. The mustiness never left the place. It always smelled the same, but that same smell is a comfort, a constant, and after all the upset I'd had this year I needed comfort more than ever.

The building is the usual long room with a stage at one end. It has a side kitchen, a loo for men and a loo for women with a rinky-dink office at the end of the corridor. For the main part, the building hasn't changed since 1923—when it was built—so the plaque on the wall reminds me. Our benefactor, John Turnbull, seated and robed, looks down on me with a benevolent smile. His smile disguises his peccadilloes. It was largely rumoured he was into young girls, very young girls, but that's another story. I took a deep breath and was rudely interrupted as the main doors were flung open and the hall flooded with bustling bodies. They all seemed to have a purpose. Like a colony of ants, each person looked incredibly busy: meeting, greeting, with arms full of precious items, jars, packages, boxes and pots paraded as they nodded to acquaintances in passing. Most were hiding anxiety beneath an exterior of superior calm.

The trestles were set up the day before, arranged by myself and Arthur whose hand brushed mine more than once. The task would normally have fallen to my husband, Bertie, but this year the mantle was thrust upon my own shoulders. I could have refused, but the allotment society was concerned Bertie's produce would go unnoticed. Rot in its grave. Well, they didn't say that of course as soil was shovelled on him only six weeks ago and Arthur only faltered towards the end of his little speech as he uttered the immortal words, 'Bertie would turn in his...err... grave if you didn't show the last of his onions!' I heard a few tuts and noticed Daphne poke him in the ribs, but I could cope.

Pristine cloths had been starched and pressed. It all looked very smart and the smell, imperceptibly changed from damp to green, enriched by vegetation as more produce wafted by. Floral structures were disrobed from their covers with a delicacy, with awe, like they were made from glass, ready to be worshipped and adored upon their altars. Many drew gasps. Not from me. I couldn't stand the competition but was happy to muck in with Bertie when he needed a piece of string cutting. String cutting to a very precise length I might add. I had to use a tape measure! I was not allowed to be a millimetre out. No, no, such was Bertie's devotion to precision.

I meandered over to the vegetable section; I had an urge to stroke the elongated parsnips, wanted to snap off little bits of Tangoed carrots, crunch them, chomp them, masticate. But it was the very straight leeks with their whitened stalks that had me blanch and I moved away. I really should back out now. Retire. Run. It was all too silly. But I had been spotted.

'Hello, Veronica!' Antonia was making her way towards me. There was no way to avoid her. I didn't think anyone could miss *her* in that voluminous floral dress and that bloody straw hat that came out every year with a new bow to match her gaudy blooms. 'I've heard you are entering Bertie's onions. How very brave of you! How wonderfully stoic!' I wanted to slap her but I was rescued by Barbara who wanted to know if I could take over tea-making duties as Yvonne was feeling poorly. She'd probably gorged on her Bath buns.

I washed cups and saucers and gazed through the window to the car park. I thought about Bertie, kind, gentle Bertie. He knew his onions; he would grow the most beautiful globes, smooth-skinned spheres that burst with flavour. Seventeen years out of the last twenty, he had won first prize. His closest rival was Horace. Horace, now retired from the town council, put all his creaking energies into organic produce. Shed-loads of equine skitter provided by Horacia, his horsey-faced offspring, was heaped on his humungous haricots. Horace was kind enough to give me a bag of this precious poo after Bertie died. Thanks Horace. I wiped my eyes. I missed the Old Stick. I turned around and managed to rope someone else in to help with the crockery and cakes. I had about half an hour left to set things up.

I could do it. I could show them. The Leadbetters could lead again! There is a voice in my head that says I'm swinging the lead but I'm not listening and unpack three pale skinned orbs with the sort of care one normally reserves for newborns. It is de rigueur to tilt one's nose upwards at this juncture and I plate them up on fine sand, tie a little blue string around their tops (I've watched Bertie do this more times than I've had hot shallots). 'They look okay – don't they?'

'What? Are you talking to me dear?'

A ruddy-faced man leaned in too close, his breath reeking of his home grown. It was Wilfred.

'Not exactly, but what do you think? Do you think they look okay? I mean, have I set them right?' It was rhetorical. They looked perfect to me.

Wilfred stroked his chin, sniffed before moving the plate a couple of inches, and declared gruffly, 'Aye, they'll do.' Thank God for a couple of inches. I moved it back when he scuttled off.

More people drifted into the hall. It was becoming claustrophobic and up on the stage I spotted Arthur watching me, perhaps with a little admiration. I think he's always had a soft spot for me and I glanced at the floor and back up at him through my lashes which I realised I'd been batting far too much. He was still watching; those terrier eyes never missed a trick and I smiled but he blanked me and moved off.

The judges were muttering – they were about to do the 'walk-around'. Arthur, Wilfred and Norman were on vegetables. Susie, Olivia and Edna were on flowers. It was always the same people on the committee even though the society had well over 200 members now. Coloured cards were shuffled. Heads nodded and shook. Discussion went on behind gnarled hands. Arthur was wagging a finger. Disagreeable chap.

A collective slump spread as the group trailed towards the marquee; competitors had half an hour to relax before the judges returned. I squeezed through to the other side of the hall. I needed to look at the competition. I needed to relax, but I was strung up like a bag of French onions and almost bit a nail before remembering I'd painted them for the occasion. I was rigid with tension and it didn't help when a hand clamped my shoulder. Thank goodness it was only Mr Cole from next door.

'How do. Thought I'd find you here. I knocked earlier. Wondered if you wanted any help. I didn't think you'd be showing anything. I thought you'd given it all away?'

'Oh, I'm fine thank you, Mr C.' I tittered, 'I kept a few back for the show. The rest has gone. I hope you enjoyed yours? How are you?'

I knew I shouldn't have asked. As much as I like my neighbour, I spent the next ten minutes trying to escape from his lumbago. And then his parting sentence left me reeling. 'I had a few of Bertie's onions. They were nice they were. Missus made a lovely soup t'other day, flavour were wonderful. It were grand. I might have it again in the week as I've got a couple left.'

I couldn't speak. He actually had a few left! He pointed, 'There's Lillian over there. Do you want to come and say hello?' He constantly rubbed his back as he spoke. I didn't care about his lumbago. I didn't care to hear any more about onion soup. I didn't care to speak to Lillian. I was so cross I could have done a Carrie.

The judges filtered in, Arthur was in prime position; women smoothed down dresses, patted their hair. I surmised cards were being placed in front of vegetables from the hush that overcame the hall, but I couldn't see. I held my breath, wanted them to walk on, wanted them to keep going, but they lingered close to mine. Bertie's. They leaned forward but I couldn't see whether they had placed me, Bertie, or not, but when heads turned in my direction and a few friends clapped, I knew we had done it. Bertie's onions had scooped first prize.

When it was all over, Arthur sauntered by, lingered by the legumes. He didn't say anything at first and I couldn't read the look on his face. He was flushed, flustered, like he was about to say something, changed his mind and walked to the end of the row. He said a few words to other competitors before sidling towards me again. He adjusted his tie. Cleared his throat.

'Well done on your win...Bertie still has it, hey?' He coughed again, 'I was in Waitrose last night,' he held a finger up, stopped me interrupting, 'they do have a wonderful vegetable selection don't they?' He looked over his shoulder and whispered, 'Not as good as ours, though?' He held his hand up again, his rheumy eyes twinkled as he added, 'I have a suggestion for you Veronica. I was wondering if you could pop over to mine sometime; I'd be very grateful if you would cast your eye over my marrow?'

Caged Bird

It was a one-Magpie kind of a day. I knew from the moment I opened my eyes it was going to be bad. Yet, what I felt now was more than sorrow. It was terror. Had I been drugged? I had no idea where I was. I wriggled frantically, tried to loosen the bonds, but it was no use, the cords that bound my wrists hurt like hell and seemed to pull tighter the more I struggled. I was face down and tried to dislodge the tape by making tiny mouth nudges against my shoulder. It was no use. I shrank into myself, sobbed. I was so cold. I tried to wipe the snot from my nose on the rough carpet beneath me but I couldn't manoeuvre my head enough without knocking against a cold metal tin—a tool-kit or something. Rags. Oil. Ropes. It stank.

******

I thought of Lauren. I'd dropped her off at school on time—at ten to nine this morning. She's started her second term on a bad note—she is barely recovered from a nasty bug–hopefully she'll manage but at least Mum is picking her up today and taking her back to hers. The school said they'll ring if necessary. I can't stop the involuntary trembling. I won't be able to answer the phone if it rings. He has it. He's taken it from me. I remember that much. I remember his hands searching my pockets. Rough pushing and shoving. Fragments were coming back to me. Bits were floating back into memory. I'd gone shopping after work. I was back about four. No one on the estate was home. I was going back to the car for another bag... I panicked, kicked out and banged my head on the metal box, cursed. I struggled again. Tried to make some noise. I had my legs free but there wasn't enough room to kick out. I heard footsteps. I moaned as loudly as I could. The footsteps were close. I couldn't breathe. It was him. He was standing outside.

The lid of the boot yawned. A blast of cold air chilled me further and I shrank into the space, wanting it to encase me. Suck me in and save me. My blind-fold slipped a little but there was nothing to see. Everywhere was black. I guessed it was around 5pm. It was pitch black. I always hated November.

'Out!' I couldn't respond with the tape over my mouth. 'Move!' He waited while I struggled to get into an upright position and on to my knees. It was impossible to clamber out with wrists firmly behind my back! I wasn't moving fast enough. He growled his impatience, grabbed my jacket and hauled me out. I fell sideways, awkwardly, one knee hitting the ground. I moaned as loudly as I could. I sensed rubble. Uneven ground. Brick.

He adjusted my blind-fold – the glimpse gave me no clues. All I knew was he had a torch, periodic flashes swept across my face. A hand pushed me in the small of my back and I stumbled along with his rough guidance. I heard cars but they were distant. At least 300 yards away. I heard nothing other than the sound of people going home. Hurrying home to warmth and comfort.

He shoved me into some sort of room, it echoed and I smelled dust. A metal door bangs shut and I hear the snap of something like a padlock. I turn towards the noise. Ears pricked. A bolt screeched across. He drags me. Left turn. Another left. Then a right. My heart hammers. I can't breathe. He speaks. The voice tells me to hush. I think he has thrown the torch down. I see a little light at my feet. He warns me not to scream, laughs to himself, mutters something like, *no one will hear anyway* and the gag is torn off along with half my skin. 'Stay still!' There is amusement in his voice. I cringe, thinking he was about to hit me as he grabs the blindfold, pulling half my hair with it. I toss my hair backwards; it is quite long, due for the hairdresser. I flick it again. My fringe is in my eyes, but I hide behind it. He steps close, his nose an inch from mine before pressing the light switch. The balaclava is terrifying. Fluorescent tubes flicker and ping into life, one after the other; a long row stretches to infinity reminiscent of The Shining. But there is nothing soft and pretty in this movie, no carpets, no pictures. Just a terrified woman and a madman. Hopefully, no axe. Breeze blocks without plaster skim extends before me. We pass doorways without doors and walk and walk and walk down a long corridor to where workmen are further on with fixtures and fittings. There are now metal doors with hatches. All shut. All grey. He pushes me on and when I dig in my heels, he drags me.

'Go on, scream. No one will hear you anyway! Scream all you want, love.'

I try it out and scream until I vomit. I can't hear him laughing through the buzzing in my ears but he finds it hilarious. He rocks backwards and forwards. His eyes like slits. Mocking. I try hard to imagine a face behind the mask. His frame is slight. The hands rough and too big for the body. He's probably young. But I know what he sounds like. He's a Scouser. One to me.

I take a deep breath. I need to think. To calm. To get him to talk. I've watched enough TV rubbish to work it out.

'Gerrin!' He grabs my arm and swings me into a room.

I'm propelled forward. It is obvious I'm in the new prison. He must be working here. He has keys. The gaoler. I'm the first inmate. I snort. I won't be the last. Someone will know him. A point to me.

'What's so funny?' He doesn't expect an answer.

'Undo my wrists.' I stand strong. Look him in the eye. 'Go on. I'm not exactly going anywhere am I?'

He stares back. Unblinking. Doesn't move.

'Go on!' I turn my back to him, presenting my wrists. It works. The bond comes off. He throws the cord on the newly screed floor.

'Don't get bossy with me girl.' He warns. 'I don't like bossy women.' He circles me. Appraising?

I stay still in the centre of the room. He is dressed in a black parka and black jeans. A cliché. Adidas trainers. Three to me. Four! I note a small tattoo on the inside of his wrist. A swirl? No, a small bird! I can talk birds.

'Did you hear the owl hoot on the way here?' He ignores me. It was a long-shot. 'Spooky creatures of the night, but I like birds.' He listened as he leaned against the wall. 'My granddad used to have an aviary. Sometimes he would let me go inside with him. Feed them. If I was a good girl.'

'Shut up!' I kept stchum whilst he skirted round me once more. He chewed the sleeve of his anorak. I knew he was out of his depth. Hadn't done this before and clearly hadn't thought it through. He was shaking and fidgeted in his pockets, before turning angrily towards me, thrusting his face in mine. 'Just keep quiet, will yous!' His breath hot on my face. Teeth not brushed for a week. Was birds his thing?

Should I try softening him further or would I make him angrier? It was worth a flutter. I had nothing to lose.

'I remember wobbling as a kid. Trying to hold out my arm with a little plastic dish of seed and dropping the stuff everywhere. The finches were lovely. Goldfinches. Really pretty little birds. Thankfully no one keeps them anymore.'

He stopped pacing, leaned against the wall and watched. I carried on.

'They were so pretty with their little red and black and yellow markings. Grandad had a real way with them. He was so calm, patient. You need patience with birds, don't you?' He closed his eyes for longer than a blink; a shift so slight it was almost imperceptible. Five to me. He nodded.

I continued, 'He must have had about fifteen at one time...'

'Stop it! I know what you are doing. It won't work. Look, just shut up and you'll get out of here. Carry on and I won't be responsible for me actions.' His right eye twitched.

That shut me up, but softly, I asked, 'Can I sit down? Please?' He nodded and I slumped to the floor. At least he was talking. Sort of. He did say, I might get out and I gave him five minutes before adding, 'My grandmother hated seeing birds in a cage. She said birds should always be able to stretch their wings. To fly.'

He flew at me, 'You think you are clever don't you? You think all this talk of birds and being free is going to get you out of here don't you?' He spewed a tormented torrent of vile, frustrated words before dropping to his knees. He held his head like he was about to pull off the balaclava. He yelled to the ceiling, hollered and kicked out. He reminded me of Lauren having a tantrum. The wall would need re-plastering. He faced me before sliding down the wall into a crumpled heap. He tried to slow his breathing, took a few deep breaths, closed his eyes and pulled his legs into a cross-legged position before reaching into his pocket for a joint.

I stayed still, tried to gauge whether dope calmed or made him excitable. I sensed the former. Sensed none of this had been thought through sufficiently. I made a stab at asserting myself and stood, hands on hips. 'What's this about? Sex? You want sex? Have it! Take it! Then let me go. I've got nothing to lose. Let's get it over with.' I pulled off my jacket, threw it down. The gauntlet.

He jumped to his feet, 'Whoah! Just a minute! I'm not a rapist!' He held his arms outstretched, palms patting the air, putting distance between us.

I guessed he was younger than me by ten years, probably about 21 or 22. Six to me. I felt further emboldened. 'What is it you want? Come on tell me. Either rape me, kill me or set me free!'

'For fuck's sake! Will you just shut up! Let me think! I'm not here to do that!'

'Well, what the hell is this about? Why am I here?' We eye-balled each other.

Neither spoke, but he blinked first. Seven. 'Come on man. Tell me!'

'Your ex.'

'I knew it!' I stopped myself from whooping. 'Tom's behind this? The bastard.'

'He said to scare yous.'

'Well, you've done that all right. Now what?' This wasn't the time for me to be too clever. Senses in overdrive. One false move...one wrong word...

'He wants to see more of Lauren. Said if he doesn't, he will create problems for yous. Said there's a court hearing coming up that will stop him seeing her or something. Look, I'm not a killer or a rapist. I owed him and I said I'd put the frighteners on yous.' This guy wanted out.

I took a deep breath. 'This is typical him–going about things the wrong way. You owe him?'

'Yeah.'

'Is he dealing again? Come on! I know all about it. Look you don't know me, but Tom is bad news. He can drag anyone into anything and before you know it– you are in a mess.'

He held his hand up. Took another drag and watched. 'I owed him. Big time. I didn't know what to do.' He scratched the back of his hands. Those large hands that were too big for his body.

'Let me guess. You couldn't pay? He was threatening you?'

'Something like that.'

'That's his style.' I got up and paced. He watched. 'This is why he doesn't get to see my daughter! This is why!' He wouldn't meet my eye but I knelt close to his face, leaned in. 'Tom is dangerous! Can't you see? You could walk away from here but it's going to get a hell of a lot worse if you do something to me!'

He took a drag. Scanned my face. His blue eyes watered.

'Go on. See that door? Open it. Keep walking. I'll follow. I don't know who you are. Where you're from. I haven't seen your face. I haven't a clue who you are. Let's leave this where it is and we both walk free. If I report this he will get banged up but you can go into hiding. What do you say? Come on man! I've got a little girl. She needs her mum. Hey? What do you say?'

He stood. His eyes were large. Frightened. He bolted. I ran after him as fast as I could. I was not going to be left inside. I wouldn't be anyone's prisoner. I watched the red lights of his car disappear, heard the squeal of rubber and walked away.

Acknowledgements

I would like to thank Sue Miller and all at TeamAuthorUK for empowering me, encouraging me and allowing me to realise getting a book out there really was a possibility.

About the Author

I have been writing and making up stories all my life. I think I started with entertaining my two younger brothers at bedtime and went on to win a competition aged 11. Seeds were sown.

Much more recently I won another competition and that set me on course to writing my first novel. I later joined a local writing group, Renegades, based in Newcastle-under-Lyme whose help in critiquing my work has been invaluable.

Rucksack Tales is a bit of fun, set mostly in The English Lakes – which is a place I love. The mountains certainly inspire me, I find walking clears the head and allows the flow of ideas. As you may have gathered, walking the fells is a real passion, an addiction! Alfred Wainwright inspired me to walk all 214 of them, completing in 2014 after an epic couple of years. I hope you enjoy my 'not-to-be-taken-too-seriously' stories.

My blog can be found on my website: **www.jmmoore.co.uk**
Facebook: JMMooreAuthor
Email: info@jmmoore.co.uk
Twitter: @fellexplorer

Coming in 2017 –
The Parting Stone